Tariq Mehmood is a prize-winning writer and film-maker. His books include *Hand on the Sun While There Is Light* and *Song of Gulzarina*. He co-directed the award-winning documentary *Injustice*. Tariq currently teaches at the American University of Beirut, in Lebanon and lives in Beirut and Manchester, UK.

YOU'RE NOT PROPER

Tariq Mehmood

HopeRoad Publishing Ltd
P O Box 55544
Exhibition Road
London SW7 2DB

www.hoperoadpublishing.com
First published by HopeRoad 2015
This edition published 2018

A CIP catalogue for this book is available from the British Library

ISBN 978-1-908446-68-8

eISBN 978-1-908446-72-5

Printed and bound by TJ international Ltd, Padstow, Cornwall, UK

YOU'RE NOT PROPER

Kiran

I live in Boarhead West. And on the other side, in Boarhead East, live the scarfies, turbans and beards. In between us, there's a great big graveyard. There used to be a textile mill where the graveyard ended - my granddad worked there. The mill's gone now. The graveyard took it over. It's where the Muslims are buried. In the middle is a roofless church, with a huge weeping willow tree near it. That's where the Willow Tree Mob, the WTM, hang out.

In this Northern English town of mine, especially during the long summer days like now, when the sun shone well into the night, I was happy. I belonged. I had my gang, and nobody bothered me. But then I woke up and couldn't work out who I was.

It all started a few weeks after my fourteenth birthday. I was hiding from Mum in my bedroom, listening to Lady Gaga on my headphones. I had a poster of her on my wall, wearing high-heeled, snake-skin shoes. A great big green snake with black stripes, almost as thick as her waist, crossed her legs and went under her back. An orange snake with black patches curled around her neck and slithered across the green one towards her waist, looping around her neck.

The poster covered half the wall opposite my bed. It was huge. It was awesome. It was perfect. It stopped my thoughts from flying out of my bedroom and banging on Donna's head and asking her, 'What did I ever do to you?'

I turned away from Lady Gaga and pushed my head into my pillow. I had washed my face so many times, trying to clean off the cross that Donna had drawn on my forehead; I could smell the soap from my pillow.

I then turned over onto my back. The crack in the ceiling that ran from one end of my bedroom to the other jeered down at me. I heard Mum come out of her room and walk down the stairs. She called out to me when she got to the bottom, but I didn't answer her. I didn't answer her. I could still see an image of Jake, standing under the willow tree, watching, just watching as Donna drew the cross on my forehead. The words she hissed rang in my ears: 'Now you are a Christian.' It hurt when she started but the pain stopped when the other girls laughed. I begged them to stop, but they just laughed and laughed. I wanted to scream but instead I laughed as well.

'Leave me alone,' I said aloud, tossing over again, hoping to chase the memories out of my head. 'You'll feel better in the morning, girl,' I assured myself.

Little did I know how wrong I would be.

It was nearly midday when I got my head out from under my quilt. Mum had knocked on the door a few times, and I had grunted in reply and gone back to sleep. Yesterday felt like a bad dream. I had forgotten to draw the curtains last night, so the sun lit up my room. A ray of light shone up on Lady Gaga.

I rubbed my forehead. I could still feel Donna's pen going up and down and across. The memory of yesterday came flooding back to me. I had wanted to get away from the heavy silence of *it*. Mum and Dad had stopped talking to each other and I had gone to see my gang. The quickest way to get to the old church was through the broken railings of the Muslim side of the graveyard. I could have walked over the railings but didn't. I took a running jump instead, stumbled and fell. As I was getting up off the ground, I heard them laugh.

Shamshad Ali, a big, busty scarfie who goes to the same school as me and who hates my guts, was pointing at me. Laila Khan was sitting next to her on a bench not far from where I had fallen and Aisha Sadiq, wearing a black tracksuit top and bottom, was doing stretches, touching the ground and standing up again.

My backside was up in the air. I stood up, brushed the dirt off my skirt and wanted to die. A sharp pain ran down my right leg. I tried not to limp but couldn't help it.

After a bit of jogging on the spot, Aisha said something to Shamshad and then ran towards me, shouldering me as she ran past and out of the graveyard.

To get to the old church I had to go on the path that went right past them. As I got closer, Shamshad stood up, blocked my way and said, 'What's with you here?'

I looked at her ugly face and wanted to say, 'Does it belong to you?' Instead, I smiled sheepishly and said, 'Nothing!'

I slowed right down, thinking, 'How could you just say, *nothing*? Why didn't you tell her, "What do you think? You think you own everything? You think you're better because you're Muslim?"'

'*Kali Gori*,' Shamshad said, sizing me up.

I stopped.

'You're white inside, aren't you?' Shamshad tutted, pointing to her arm. 'But brown, like me.'

I kept quiet.

Shamshad came towards me, saying, 'Oreo.'

'I like Oreos.' I knew I shouldn't have said this even as the words came out of my mouth.

Shamshad looked at Laila and the two of them laughed. I didn't find anything funny but I laughed as well. Just then, I caught a glimpse of Donna and the gang. I waved at them. Shamshad stepped aside and I ran past her.

No one in the gang greeted me when I got to them. Jake stood on his own, under the flowing branches of the tree, kicking the trunk gently. Megan and Chloe stood on either side of Donna. Megan had her arms folded across her chest and Chloe played with a twirl of her blonde hair. Donna glared at me like I was dirt.

'Alright, Don?' I asked.

Megan scratched her back and gaped at Donna.

Donna ignored me and nodded for Megan and Chloe to follow her; they walked towards a hedge close to me. I went up to Jake and asked, 'What's with everyone?'

He grabbed hold of a small branch in his fist and stripped the leaves off it.

'Ouch, that must have hurt, Jake,' I said.

'It's our Dex,' Jake said, tossing the leaves to the ground.

Before he could say anything else, Donna pushed Laila through the hedge and came out holding Shamshad by the wrist. Laila stumbled and fell. Ripping the hijab off Shamshad's head, Donna said, 'Spying on us, eh?'

'Oh please don't,' Shamshad cried, trying to get the hijab back. 'Me Dad'll kill me!'

'Me Dad'll kill me!' Chloe mimicked, snatching the hijab from Donna and waving it just out of Shamshad's reach.

Donna's impersonation of Shamshad, especially with her Pakistani accent, was so good I couldn't help but laugh.

I laughed all the louder remembering what Shamshad had said to me earlier.

'Stop it, Donna,' Jake said, coming out from under the tree. 'Give it back to her.'

Donna ignored Jake, just as she had ignored me, and kept waving the hijab in front of Shamshad. 'I said give it back to her,' Jake repeated, stepping towards Donna.

Donna stared at Jake for a moment and then screwed up the hijab and threw it into a bush. As Shamshad retrieved her hijab, Laila told Donna, 'You're just a coward at heart, aren't you?'

Donna clenched her fists and turned towards Laila. I had seen her batter people when she was like this. I quickly stepped in between her and Laila, and said, 'That's enough, Donna.'

Donna grabbed me by the shoulders, and hissed, 'Whose side are you on?'

As I stepped away from Donna, I saw Shamshad and Laila run down the path away from us.

When they were out of sight, Donna held up a pretend gun and pointed it towards me, saying, 'Bang! Bang! Bang!'

'What's up with everyone?' I sighed.

Donna put her hand into her trouser pocket, pulled out a photograph and squatted onto the ground. She kissed the photograph and started crying.

Megan went up to Donna, took the photograph from her hand, came over to me and held it close to my face. It was of Donna's boyfriend, Jake's brother Dex, in army uniform posing with a gun.

Donna stood up, pointed the pretend gun at me again and said, 'You Taliban have got my Dex and if anything happens to him, you're dead, Paki.'

'Let up, Don,' I said.

'You're Muslamic, aren't you, *Karen*?' Megan sneered.

'I'm one of us,' I said, turning to Jake, hoping he would take my side. He just looked at me, a look I had not seen before. Like he was looking at someone he didn't know. 'And it's Islamic or Muslim, not Muslamic,' I added.

'It's all the same, innit?' Donna glared at me and asked, 'You're really one of them, aren't you?'

My stomach knotted.

'Com' on, say it then,' Megan said, poking me in the chest with her finger.

'I'm not a Muslim,' I said and then I laughed falsely. I wanted to say, 'None of us in the Willow Tree Mob believe in God any road,' but instead, I said, 'And unlike you, I go to church, at least sometimes.'

Holding the small silver crucifix around her neck, Donna pointed at me with her fat finger and asked, 'Where's yours?'

Everyone just stared at me. I was frightened and as I made to leave, Chloe blocked my way, saying, 'You're not proper, not like us.' Her freckly, pink face was a burning red.

'I am. I'm proper, just like you,' I said, choking on my words.

'I'll make you proper.' Donna grabbed my wrist. She towered over me. Megan held me by the shoulders and Chloe pushed my arm up my back.

'Jake!' I called out.

He ignored me and went back under the tree.

That was when I felt Donna's pen digging into my forehead. I don't know how long she rubbed it into my skin, but she stopped when I noticed Shamshad and a load of hijab-wearing girls coming towards us. Donna, Megan and Chloe scampered away immediately.

The sound of a song from prehistoric times chased yesterday's nightmare out of my mind. Someone was playing 'Lovely Day'.

Throwing the quilt off me, I sat up in bed and looked around my bedroom. My school jacket was hanging on the back of my door, not on the floor where I had dumped it. My skirt and socks were in the wash basket and not by the side of my bed. The music outside got louder and I said to Lady Gaga's poster, 'It's not your type.'

My mobile buzzed. I tried to remember where I had put it. I saw it flashing in my jacket pocket. By the time I got to it, it stopped. I had four missed calls from Jake and one text. I read the text: *Sorry for what they did to you.*

Clenching the mobile tightly in my hand, I felt like throwing it against the wall. Instead, I replied to Jake: *U?* Jake replied before I got back into bed: *I did nthng.*

Me: *Yeh nthng.*

I waited for Jake's reply and then I wrote: *Lol.*

And then I sent another message: *A Paki eh. Lol.*

My eyes began to burn and blur as I sent another: *Cross me forehead+hope 2 die. Lol.*

I dropped the mobile on the floor and pulled the quilt over my head. The telephone started buzzing. I picked it up, pulled the quilt over my head and read it. It was Jake. I rejected the call.

He rang again and I answered this time. 'What you do want?'

'You know our Dex is missing out there, don't you?'

'I know now. It's writ on me for'head, isn't it. Besides, I didn't ask him to go, did I!'

'And you know what I think? I didn't want him to go. I hate this war. You know I hate it. I told him "I don't want you to go..."'

But I'd had enough of Jake and disconnected the call.

He immediately sent a message: *Sorry.*

I replied: *Lol.*

He replied: *C u @school.*

I replied: *H8 u.*

I sent another: *All of you,* before turning the mobile off.

'*Karen*, you're really one of the gang now, aren't you, girl?' I said aloud, taking my head out from under the quilt. 'Islamic, Muslamic.' I thought about how I had laughed at the way the gang made fun of the hijab-wearing women. I then felt very guilty as I remembered how I had laughed when Jake had gone up to a man with a long beard and a turban, and said, 'Run for your wives.'

I frowned, and could feel the pain coming back in my forehead. I knew now, I never did belong to the WTM, my gang. They never saw me as I saw them. I never saw *me* as they saw me. I thought I was just me. And who was I? Mixed-race? Oreo? Christian? Muslim?

The image of Donna and the gang fleeing at the sight of Shamshad and the hijab-wearing girls flashed through my mind. I felt a pang of jealousy. They knew who they were. They belonged. They believed. They didn't need to pretend to be anything, they just were. And me, what was I? I certainly wasn't what I thought I was. What a messed-up family I had. A Muslim Dad who loved beer and bacon and a Christian Mum who didn't believe in God, but went to church.

I lay in bed thinking back to how Mum used to take me to church on Sundays. How beautiful she looked in her flowery red dresses, with her blonde hair falling on her shoulders and her thin nose. She wore a silver nose stud, which she only put on when going to church, one Dad had bought her when they had first met - and the story of which she always ended with the sly remark, 'If Man U had not won, I am sure he would never have bought this for me.'

Sometimes, getting ready for church, I would stare at my own nose in the mirror. It was thin, but no matter if I looked at it a thousand times and told myself it looked like hers, it just didn't. And whenever I asked her about this, she would go silent for a moment, as though I had asked her the most difficult question in the world and then squeeze my nose, saying, 'It doesn't matter, dear. You have the loveliest nose in the whole wide world.'

Mum's chin is beautiful and perfectly round and I hate mine. It's pointy and too long. Mum's eyebrows are so perfect, she never needs to have them plucked and mine grow so fast, one day I'll need a hedge trimmer.

At church she would smile at this person and laugh with that one, her green eyes lighting up each time, like she had not seen them for ages. She once told me she got her eyes from her Dad and blonde hair from her Mum. But I never did see these grandparents of mine. They died before I was born, Mum said. They were upset with my Mum 'cause they didn't want her to marry my Dad. They didn't think much of Pakistanis. But Mum loved my Dad. Even though he's a slob, my Dad, Mum still loves him.

The last time I went to church with Mum, Dad was fidgeting about in the living room. Looking at us, he sniggered, 'And say hello to *Him* and His son.'

Mum cleared her throat, letting out a disapproving, 'Ahm.'

'Stop filling me daughter's head with all this rubbish,' Dad said, as we were about to leave the house.

Mum looked at me, grinned, flicked her eyes, shook her head, and then shouted back to Dad, 'Make sure you keep an eye on the chicken, it's simmering.'

'Not going to lay an egg now, is it?' Dad replied.

In church we stood in our usual place, in the last aisle near the door, holding our hymn books, but as soon as we started singing the first hymn, 'Onward, Christian Soldiers', Mum grabbed my hand and whispered. 'I hate this one,' and led me out of church. I was glad.

When we got home Dad was stomping around in the kitchen.

'I bet he burnt the chicken,' Mum said to me.

'I turned it off, before you ask,' Dad said, coming out of the kitchen, rubbing his head in both his hands.

He had curry stains on his white vest, which he had clearly tried to wipe off, smudging it all the more.

Mum folded her arms in front of her, smiling one of her *herehegoesagain* sort of smiles and nudged me in the ribs.

As Dad was about to leave the kitchen, Mum said, 'Well, Lucky, aren't you going to ask how it was?'

'How was it?' Dad asked, opening the door to the living room. The television was on. And what else would he be watching but football?

'Aren't you a bundle of laughs to come back to,' Mum smirked, following him.

I loved moments like this, with Mum and Dad. They were such kids.

'Aren't you going to ask your daughter how it was for her?'

'How was it, Karen?' Dad asked, placing his elbows on the coffee table, his chin in his hands and his eyes fixed on the television screen.

'We left just when the first hymn started,' I said.

'Go on, sweetheart, sing it for your Dad, you know it by heart.'

'No.'

'Go on, dear, you know how much I love seeing him like this,' Mum breathed into my ear and then gave me one of those great big smiles, which meant that if I did what she asked, then there were a lot of brownie points for me.

I started singing: 'Onward, Christian soldiers, marching as to war, With the cross of Jesus going on before.'

'Oh God, why this,' Dad snapped and stood up. When he turned around, he was white with rage. His fist clenched.

Mum pushed me behind her, saying, 'Lucky, don't you bloody well dare.'

I thought Dad was going to hit Mum. I had never seen him like this. He stood there shaking. After a moment, he pointed at the television screen and said, 'City are at the top of the league.'

I slid out of bed, went into the bathroom and looked at myself in the mirror. I was a flat-chested, brown girl with a thin nose. I screamed, thinking, 'Who are you?'

The girl looking back at me had shoulder-length, curly black hair. She had black pupils and thick eyebrows. Her arms were like her face, brown with black hair on them.

This wasn't me. I must be dreaming, I thought, and slapped myself on the face. I felt numb.

I screamed again, and this time I couldn't stop.

Mum came rushing upstairs, soapsuds dripping off her yellow rubber gloves, 'What's up, dear?' she asked.

I heard Dad jumping out of bed.

I placed my arm next to Mum's white-skinned arm. 'I didn't turn out like *you*!' I cried. 'I'm not white, Mum!'

Mum gave me a hug, kissed me on the head, saying, 'It doesn't matter, Karen dear. I love you all the same.'

'My name's not Karen, is it, Mum?'

'Did someone hurt you, Karey?' Mum wanted to know.

'No,' I said. 'It's not Karey, is it, Mum?'

Touching my forehead Mum frowned and said, 'What happened here?'

'It's not Karey, is it?' I asked again.

Mum didn't say anything back.

'What happened, Karen?' Dad asked, rubbing his eyes.

I saw Dad's reflection in the mirror. He was wearing a white vest and tartan boxer shorts. The vest was crumpled up over his big belly. His greying chest hair stuck out of the vest towards his chin and stomach. He had really hairy arms and hands. His eyes were bloodshot.

'My name is Kiran, Dad. It's Kiran and not Karen, isn't it?'

Dad looked at my Mum. They exchanged a *whatssheonabout* look. 'Your daughter says she's not white,' Mum said to Dad. I could tell they were having a hard time keeping a straight face.

'Neither am I, sweety,' Dad said. 'You look just like me.'

'Oh god Dad, I don't want to look like *you*,' I said.

Mum ran her hand across my face, wiping my tears. Dad went back to his bedroom holding his forehead.

Mum gave me a *don'tyouworry* type of a hug. Dad snored. Mum and I looked at each other and laughed. She kissed me on the head and went downstairs. I went to my bedroom and ripped the poster of Lady Gaga off the wall; tore it into pieces and shoved it into the bin next to my wardrobe.

Dad snored even louder.

Yep, they're right, I thought. *I've got a sort of Muslim Dad.*

'Well, Dad you can drink and snore your way out of your religion, but I can't get you out of me,' I said aloud. 'Help me find me, Dad. I need you.' Just then, Dad let out the loudest snore I had ever heard from him.

I looked at the back of my hand. It was brown. I turned it over and my palm was a lighter brown, with little splotches and three lines curving down the middle. I saw the faces of my gang flash in front of me: Jake looking at me with his blue eyes, Donna glaring at me, her double chin wobbling, the airhead Megan nodding and Chloe shaking her hair out of her face. They didn't see me. I was buried somewhere in a mosque behind my brown skin. 'Well, gang,' I thought, 'I am Kiran Malik and I am what I am. That is what I am and there is no getting away from it for me.' '

And what are you?' I asked aloud and I answered myself, 'I am going to find out where I belong.' And I thought of Shamshad. I felt pride thinking about her gang, even though they hated me. They were right to hate me. I hated myself.

I grabbed my CDs and flung them towards the bin, one by one. Some hit their target; others hit the wall. 'What's music got to do with it?' I said to myself. 'And besides, *Karen* spent a lot of her pocket money there.'

I picked up the CDs. Some of the cases had cracked. Putting the CDs back made me feel better. When they were all back in their positions, I pointed at them and said, 'When I'm ready, I'll get rid of some of you, so make sure you behave!'

I touched my forehead. It still hurt, a strange sort of hurt that went deep down, right down to where I was hiding from myself. 'Well, Kiran,' I thought, 'whoever is hiding behind this skin is not a Christian.'

I don't know how long I faffed about in my bedroom. When I went down, Mum was wiping invisible dust off our immaculately clean kitchen worktop.

My Mum is not like normal Mums who tell you to tidy up after yourself. Mine has a place for everything and everything has its place, especially on one of those days when the East Boarhead Curry Club come round. That's Mum's new hobby. She teaches our neighbours how to make authentic curry. In the curry club, there's old George from next door, and snooty Elizabeth from number 31, and one or two other dinosaurs.

'Are you feeling better, dear?' Mum asked, wiping the inside of the sink.

'Mum, can I talk to you? There's a lot I want to say.'

Mum rinsed the cloth and replied, 'Course you can, love.'

Mum stopped, let out a sigh, rinsed the cloth and hung it on a tap to dry.

'Why did you take me to church, Mum?' I wept.

'I didn't want you to turn out like me or your Dad, dear,' Mum said, looking very sad. 'If I had faith, this pain inside me, maybe it wouldn't hurt so much, maybe it wouldn't hurt at all. Sometimes it hurts so bad, I just don't want to live, just can't take it anymore.' She covered her eyes with her hand and said brokenly, 'Oh my love, I should have held you tighter. How could I have let you go?'

'What pain, Mum?' I wanted to ask. 'Held who, Mum? Please Mum, tell me what is this secret that you and Dad are keeping from me, this thing that comes like a terrifying shadow of silence over our house?'

She would never tell me and I was always too scared to ask. Whatever it was, I had to find out; without this missing knowledge, I couldn't find me. I didn't know then that my search to find me would destroy both my family and my world.

She looked at me with eyes that hid behind a coldness that came on when *it* took hold of her, but today, her eyes were rolling, as if she was fighting to stave *it* off, now winning, now losing. Her face went pale, ghost-like and then her colour returned.

'I never want to go to church again, Mum. I don't feel Christian, I just don't. I don't know what I want but I don't want to be what I am. I hate my gang now, Mum. I don't want to be like them. I'm something else. I want to have faith like you used to say. And I've decided I want to be a Muslim. That's how I feel, Mum.'

Mum untied her stripy blue apron, took it off her and said, 'That's nice, dear.'

I suddenly felt a rush of hatred for Mum and said, choking on my words, 'Don't you care what happens to me, Mum?'

'Of course I do. I love you!.'

'Is that it? That's all you have to say?'

Hanging the apron on a hook on the back door, Mum turned around and gave me a look, which said, *you'rejustastupidkid.* 'If you want to try Islam for a while, that's OK, sweetheart.'

'Oh Mum, it's not a game. I'm really, really serious,' I cried.

Mum snapped out of her mood, kissed me on the cheeks, held my face in her hands and said, 'I love you because I love you for being you.'

Hugging Mum I thought of me walking into school wearing a hijab. I knew they were going to laugh at me when they first saw me wearing a headscarf. But I didn't care. I was going to wear it. That was how it was going to be.

Pulling away from me, Mum said, 'I think you should talk to your Dad.'

'I know, Mum.' Then I said, 'Love you.'

Dad was in his usual place in the living room.

'How do I become a Muslim?' I asked Dad, walking into the living room.

'Yes pet, you can. Take a fiver from me wallet.' Dad was glued to a football match he was watching on television.

'You don't know what I need Dad,' I said.

'Alright, pet...'

'I'm not your pet, Dad,' I said, gritting my teeth.

'Alright, you can have a tenner,' he said, waving his hand in the air.

Mum stood behind me. I stomped over and stood in between the telly and Dad, and said, 'How do I become a Muslim?'

He looked at me in bewilderment, then at my Mum, and they exchanged a *whatnow* type of look.

'You don't know, do you, Dad?' I said.

Dad shuffled his bum on the settee. 'You don't, do you?' I repeated.

'He doesn't,' Mum said. 'His real God's football, really. And if Mohammed the Prophet played for Manchester

United, then you'd have known everything, wouldn't you, Lucky?' she jibed.

'Less of the tongue, Sharon. And since when did you start believing in all that Holy Mother stuff?' Dad said. 'Apart from Guinness, the only decent thing you Catholics have come up with is Man U.'

'You really don't know a thing, do you, Dad?'

He turned the television off, rubbed his hand through his thick curly hair, and said, 'Course I do.'

Pointing to the sofa opposite him, he told me, 'Sit there.'

I did. Mum came and sat next to me. I wanted Mum to say something, to say no, she had tried to turn me into a Christian. Then I would tell her what was really, really on my mind- but she just stayed silent. I said to her, 'You're not bothered what I become, are you?'

Mum and Dad looked at each other coldly, like they were about to fight. Like *it* was going to start right now and Mum would turn into a ghost. I didn't care.

Mum took a deep breath and sighed, 'I just want you to be happy, Kiran.'

'You're lying,' I said. 'You've always lied to me.'

'All you have to do is believe in Allah,' Dad said.

'That's just God.'

'Yeh,' said Dad. 'I can teach you more later.'

Mum put her hand in front of her mouth. I couldn't tell if she was laughing or crying.

'But what do I have to do to become a Muslim?'

'You have to recite the *Kalmas*,' Dad said, 'as a start, like.'

He then recited the *Kalma*, '*La ilaha, illallah, Muhammad ur Rasoolullah*.' He looked a bit unsure of himself, and said, 'It means: There is no God but Allah, and Mohammad is his prophet.'

'Are you sure, Dad?'

'Yeh, pretty much. It's something like that.'

Mum left the room.

I tried to repeat what Dad said but kept forgetting.

Dad went back to the television, and I left to buy my first hijab. As I was leaving the house, Mum stood by the front door and looked at me.

'What is it, Mum?'

She just looked at me with eyes that seemed to flicker between different worlds, one where she saw me and the other where I couldn't see her. Her blonde hair was held back by a black ribbon. It was the first time I noticed streaks of grey in her hair. The lines on her forehead twitched. She didn't look like the strong woman she was, always knowing what had to be done and when.

'Dinner'll be ready when you get back, Kiran,' she said.

It was bright and sunny outside, with a slight chill in the air. A few drops of rain came down out of a cloudless sky. Our neighbour, old George, sat in his front garden with Bruno, his dog, near him. I waved to him and George nodded to me.

Getting out of our gate, I said a loud 'Hi' to Elizabeth, our other neighbour. She was coming towards me, holding the leash of her poodle, which was a few steps behind her, cocking its leg near a broken street lamp. She lifted her chin to make sure I knew she had been to the hairdresser and smiled back at me. I stepped onto the road. There were so many unfilled holes in it nowadays, ever since the last freaky cold winter a couple of years back, when, after the snow melted, the tarmac had cracked, so everyone drove really carefully.

I turned left and crossed the road close to where a car had been burnt. Some older boys were sitting in the carcass, taking turns smoking a large, hand-rolled cigarette and eyeing me. I felt like sticking my finger up at them, and telling them to go get a job, instead of doing this all day. But there weren't any jobs round here.

They were still eyeing me up so I quickened my pace. I didn't really know where I was going to get my hijab from, but as there were plenty of shops in East Boarhead, I was sure to find one. The quickest way to get there was through the graveyard, but I didn't want to bump into anyone so went the long way round, along St. Enoch's Road, past boarded-up shops and derelict houses with broken windows. The road snaked around the cemetery and changed into Market Road as it got closer to the city centre.

At the junction where the new road began there were a group of shops I hadn't noticed before. I stopped outside the window of a shop called 'Cluck-Cluck'. A shop worker, a small white woman, was dressing a female mannequin in blue lacy underwear. The dummy was wearing a shiny, white hijab. I was giggling at the sight of the mannequin when a tall woman dressed in flowing black robes stopped close to me and looked at the same mannequin. Apart from her eyes, everything else about her was covered. She even wore black gloves. She walked into the shop and I went in after her.

Inside the shop, she went up to the mannequin that was being dressed and felt the underwear. As she was doing this, the shop worker pointed to a stand and said, 'They're over there.'

The woman in black walked over to the stand, picked some underwear and went to the counter to pay.

I went to the back of the store, chose a couple of hijabs from a pile in a wooden basket and stood behind the woman in black to pay. She turned round to me and said, 'And less of those dirty looks, young lady.'

When I got home with my hijabs, the East Boarhead Curry Club, pans in hand, were walking into our house. Old George, with his violin case dangling off his shoulder, was at the back. Once they were in, I carefully closed the door and tried to sneak upstairs, unnoticed. I avoided the first step, as it squeaked, and had just put my foot on the next one when Mum called, 'Kiran, sweetheart, can you come here?'

I pretended not to hear her and took another step.

'Come on love, I know you heard me,' Mum called again. I really dreaded moments like this.

'Mum, please, can't Dad do it this time,' I yelled back.

'No one trusts his judgement,' Mum replied.

I stomped into the kitchen, folded my arms in front of me, still holding my shopping bag, and hissed, 'What?!'

Old George as ever was in his white trainers, yellow shorts and a matching, sleeveless sweatshirt. He had a great, big, proud smile across his ugly, bony face. He tapped on his creation, which was in an oblong, silver pan. Next to George stood Elizabeth, her ridiculous brown hat with small plastic flowers still on her head and whatever she was cooking in a reddish-brown baking bowl, whose lid was in the shape of a flower. And next to Elizabeth was a flat, round woman, in a fading black skirt and a fading black blouse. I didn't know her name but everyone called her the 'bulldog' and kept away from her. Her pink, chubby face was all blotchy. Each time she moved, the flab under her chin wobbled. She stood behind a tall, stainless steel pan. Mum was leaning against the sink. Someone's cat was perched outside in the garden behind Mum.

'Please Mum, not again,' I pleaded, with my stomach turning at the thought of what was about to befall me.

'Your Mum's such a good curry cooker, she is,' George said, rubbing his tongue over what few teeth he had left. He touched the lid of his pan and added, 'I've made a special doo peeza, I have.'

I trembled.

'You know that dish, don't you?' George asked me and then he answered himself, 'course you do.'

'It's do peeaaza, George,' Mum corrected him.

'I've forgotten exactly what it means, like,' George said, scratching his shiny, bald head.

'Two onions,' Mum reminded him.

'Two onions!' George raised his silver eyebrows, his clean-shaven face twitching. 'Oh, dear.'

'Double onion, you idiots,' Dad shouted from the living room.

'Double Onion!' George repeated, a look of bewilderment on his face.

'I hate onions, Mum, you know I hate them,' I protested.

'Oh my,' George sighed, lifting the lid off his pan.

I could have just died at the sight of his creation. It was something sickly reddish-yellow, with lumps in it.

'I thought it meant double vindaloo,' George said meekly.

'What's that?' I snapped.

Mum put her hand to her mouth, her eyes laughing.

'Cornflake do peeaaza, that's what it's meant to be, like,' he said.

'You daft git,' Elizabeth said, lifting the lid of her pan, 'you can't make cornflake curry. I made chicken tikka masala.'

The only way you could tell that Elizabeth's creation was once a chicken was from the burnt drumsticks, which were almost completely black, floating in a gooey, brown sauce.

I dropped my arms to my sides and yelped. I was about to leg it out of the kitchen when Mrs Bulldog stirred and lifted the lid of her pan. A rich aroma of freshly chopped coriander mixed with the smell of spices and lentils filled the kitchen. She smiled and said in a soft voice, 'I used real ghee and lots of fresh garlic for the garnish. I think you should taste mine first, love.'

'It all looks delicious, you know,' I said, throwing Mum another pleading look.

Mum flicked her eyebrows and nodded, freeing me from my ordeal. Just then, Mrs Bulldog put her nose up at George and said, 'I bet you wouldn't dare feed it to your dog, George.'

'I already have and he loved it,' George interjected.

They all burst out laughing and I bolted out of the kitchen, thanking my lucky stars.

I had hardly got into my bedroom when I heard Mum running upstairs. I dived onto my bed and quickly got under the quilt, but Mum hadn't come for me and went into her own room. Just then, George starting playing a jig on the violin downstairs. I cringed and shouted from under the quilt, 'Oh, God save me!'

'You coming, love?' Mum said, entering into my room.

I kept my head under the quilt and didn't answer. Downstairs, the violin was now being accompanied by clapping and the muffled curses of Dad.

'Come on, love,' Mum said.

I lifted the quilt off my head and there was Mum, wearing a green dress with black stockings and her black dancing shoes; her hair was neatly brushed and was held in place by a green hairband across her forehead. 'What's up, Mum?'

'It's such a lovely day...'

'But what's with the dancing?' I interrupted.

Holding her hands straight by her sides, Mum started dancing, her feet beating a perfect rhythm on my bedroom floor.

Mum looked like a little girl skipping. She danced out of my room and down the stairs. I followed, I just had to see what Dad made of all this. It was a match day.

He was standing by the door of the living room tapping his feet.

Elizabeth was twirling round and the flab on Mrs Bulldog was doing a frenzied dance to the tune of George's jig.

'Can't you play anything other than Morrison's jig, George?' Dad asked.

George just grinned and carried on playing. He suddenly looked years younger.

In the morning, Mum left for work at Asda. She did the early shift on Mondays. I lay in bed a bit longer than I should have. I kept thinking about what everyone would say at school. Finally, I jumped up, got dressed, put my headscarf on, ran downstairs, wolfed down some cornflakes and bolted out of the door.

On the bus to school, a few girls gave me the evil eye, but I ignored them. This was the first time I wasn't worried about meeting Shamshad. I was going to tell her I knew the

Kalma and I was sorry for everything that had happened in the past. This was the new me and I'd like us to be friends.

I got off the bus reciting the *Kalma* to myself when she jumped out of the old warehouse. I was startled, but that was nothing compared to what I felt when I realised what I had done.

I looked down at my legs and realised what Shamshad was looking at: me, wearing a black hijab, a white shirt, a school tie, a black blazer, a short, black skirt, and white socks. I turned round to run back home and ran into Aisha Sadiq. Laila was close by.

'Push her to me, Laila,' Shamshad said.

Laila didn't touch me.

'Whose side are you on, Laila?' Shamshad asked, grabbing me.

Shamshad called everyone towards her, and I was trapped in the middle of a circle. Their mouths were wide open. I dropped my arms by my side. They were really heavy. She spun me round. I kept thinking, 'You deserve everything you get, Kiran.' The whole world was laughing at me. And so it should. Shamshad was pointing her mobile phone at me to take a picture. Mixed-up rubbish, that's all I was, trash. You're right Shamshad, and you're right Laila, and every one of you. How could I do this to you?

I don't know what happened. All of a sudden everyone just vanished. I turned around and walked, not knowing where I was going.

Shamshad

I had gone to the graveyard with my friend Laila to see the new headstone on my granddad's grave. May the Almighty grant him a place in Heaven. It was made of royal white marble, with the *Kalma* carved into it, running around its flowery edge. Someone had written 'EDL' on the last one. We were sitting on a bench under one of the new CCTV cameras, which covered our graveyard, when Karen Malik came flying over the fence and landed on her bum not far from us.

What else can you do but laugh at someone whose behind is stuck up in the air and whose knickers have gone up their bum?

'I can't stand people like her,' I said loudly to Laila. 'Especially when she's sucking up to her *gora* gang.'

'Oh, Shami,' Laila protested, squeezing my hand, 'let's not let her spoil it.'

'Look what the cat's brought in,' Aisha said as Karen was about to jog. I nodded, letting out a sigh of relief, but still couldn't help thinking about how her gang had made me feel so bad, so often; how they had humiliated me because I'm Muslim, especially that Donna.

'You know, Laila, once when I went past her gang, Donna started singing, "God made little brown people. He made 'em in the night. He made 'em in a hurry and forgot to paint 'em white."'

'It's stupid,' Laila laughed.

'It is a bit, but then I didn't think it was funny, you know. What really got under my nose was the way Karen laughed with them.'

'What a cow,' Laila said.

'*Qasmein*, I swear. Isn't she just.'

After Karen went to see her gang, Laila and I strolled up the path to see what she was going to do.

I didn't see them coming. They jumped up from behind us. Donna pushed Laila through the hedge. She held my wrists so tightly in her fat hand it hurt. I wish I had said nothing to her, just punched her in the face when she ripped off my hijab, but ended up saying the most stupid thing in the world, 'Me Dad'll kill me!'

I don't know why, but when that Chloe was waving my hijab in front of my face, pretending somehow I talked like that, it made me think about her seventh birthday party. She was so excited she couldn't blow the candles out, so I blew them out for her and she ran to me and hugged me.

What made me really, really mad was the way Karen joined in laughing at me. It's one thing leaving Islam for her Mum's religion, but it's another ganging up with her WTM posse and insulting mine. It's just as well they ran off when I came back with the girls. On the way back home, I said to Laila, 'I'm going to teach that *Karen* a lesson tomorrow, she'll never ever forget.'

I prayed inside my head, '*Ya Allah*, give me strength to get my own back on her.'

I couldn't even keep Karen out of my dreams that night, when I slept. I dreamed I was going to a special assembly at school. Everyone was there. There was only one chair left empty. It was in the front of the hall. Everyone was looking at me. Karen was standing next to me, her eye on the chair. I ran for the chair. Everyone cheered. She ran for the same chair. I grabbed her hand, to pull her back but she snatched it free and beat me to the chair. The teachers were praising her. Everyone was clapping for her and laughing at me. My mother stood at the back of the hall. Stone-faced, as ever. I ran to her, crying. I held my arms out for Mum to hug me. She folded her arms. I ran past her and just as I got outside the assembly hall, there was Karen and her mother. Her white mother, combing Karen's hair.

The next morning, I put a pair of scissors in my bag and caught the bus to school early to wait for Karen.

After getting off the bus at our school stop, Karen usually went to Gilani's to get a drink. The shop was next to an ivy-covered abandoned warehouse at the end of a street full of 'For Sale' signs. I was going to grab Karen, pull her into the warehouse, and give her a hiding she would never forget. I was going to cut her hair and rub muck in her face.

I saw her bus coming, grabbed some muck and hid. She was muttering something to herself. I held my breath and then jumped in front of her. She yelled like she had seen a ghost. I grabbed her by the throat and pulled her towards me. I shoved some of the dirt right into her mouth and rubbed it into her face. As I pulled the scissors out of my bag, I saw Laila coming towards us. I let go of Karen and laughed and laughed at the sight of her. Not at how dirty her face looked, though that was hilarious, but at what she was wearing.

'Look at you!' I cried, pointing to her legs.

Karen looked down and went white. She turned around to leave, but Aisha was right behind her.

As I was leaving school, I stared at a poster of our Halloween party, a copy of which was stuck on either side of the exit door. It said: *Cum On Yea Ghouls, Vamps and Bats.* Against a yellow background were black outlines of witches flying about on broomsticks and bats of all shapes and sizes. Underneath these in thick gothic letters was written #freakyfriday.

I left school that day, flushed with happiness, made all the better by a bright October day. Walking out of the doors, I thanked *Allahjee* for giving me a chance to get my own back on Karen.

I just couldn't get comfortable in the bus seat on the way home; I had a prickly pain in my bum and kept moving about. I could feel a spot or a lump. It hurt each time I pressed down on it.

As soon as I got off the bus, I rushed back home to help Mum. Dad was having one of his parties. They always took place on a Monday. I hated these parties. It was usually the same old men, saying the same old things and leaving their same old smells behind.

There are no pictures on any walls in my house. Dad has forbidden them. Un-Islamic, they are. There is no music. No television. Not allowed. I am allowed a computer, though. Dad got it for my fourteenth birthday. It turned out to be more of a gift for my mother than me!

Though she can't read or write, she's learned to turn the computer on and use Skype. She's always online, gabbing away with her family in Pakistan. She shuts the door if she knows I'm around. Usually, she looks all shrivelled up, but talking to someone in Pakistan on Skype, she seems to grow taller, pointing at the screen and shaking her head.

When I got home, Mum was looking at a darkish, grainy figure of a woman on the computer screen. She didn't realise I was back. 'How many goats did I give you to look after?' Mum asked.

'Ten,' the dark woman replied.

'How many have you got now?'

'Nine.'

'What happened to the missing goat?'

The dark woman went quiet for a moment and then said, 'The Khyber Express went over her.'

I dropped my bag in the hallway. Hearing me, Mum shut the door and continued. 'What were you doing?' Mum was furious. She swore.

'I was bringing my animals back from the jungle,' the other woman said. 'I have twenty-six goats and four cows.'

'Which one of my goats died?'

'The soil-coloured one with white patches.'

'Didn't that one give birth only three months ago?' Mum asked.

'And it was pregnant again.'

'What happened to the offspring?'

'One of them was born without eyes, and a wolf took the other one.'

'How is it that it's always my goats that the wolf takes, that it's only my goats that go under the Khyber Express?

I could hear people in the room in Pakistan laugh when she said this. Just then, the Skype connection went. 'Load-shedding. Always load-shedding when I want to talk.' Mum cursed the electricity people in Pakistan.

She came out of the front room, nodded to me and disappeared towards the kitchen at the back of the house.

I put my school bag on the table near the stairs, took off my shoes, placed them on the shoe rack and went upstairs.

I ran the bath and watched steam from the water rising. Wiping our big bathroom mirror, for a moment I felt a shock run through my body when I thought I saw Karen's long, bony face in my reflection in the mirror.

'Get out of my head, you cow,' I snarled, looking closely at my own reflection. Was this chubby face with thick eyebrows really me?

I could hear Mum and Dad talking about something outside the bathroom door, but couldn't work out what they were saying to each other.

I got hold of Dad's round shaving mirror and looked at what was causing me so much pain. It was a ginormous boil and without thinking, I shouted, 'Dad, I've got a boil on my bum.'

'That's OK. I've got one on my bum as well.'

Mum and Dad laughed out loud, a rare thing in our house. When they finished laughing, and they laughed for a long time, Dad said, 'I'm popping out to the shops. Do you want anything, Shamshad?'

I didn't reply. In our house you never talked to someone in the bathroom, let alone what I had just said, and to Dad at that. I felt so ashamed. I got into the bath, lowered my head and watched my hair spreading in the water.

After having my bath and getting changed, I ran downstairs and went straight into the kitchen. Mum was chopping onions. I called out for my cat and listened for the patter of her feet coming down the stairs. She loved curling up in a basket in my bedroom.

'She's not been in all day,' Mum said, putting the chopped onions into a plastic bowl.

'All day!' I exclaimed. 'She must be really hungry.'

Mum didn't say anything at first. As I bent down to pick up a half-empty packet of cat food she said, 'Hungry animals find food. Or they die trying to find it.'

I didn't say anything to her. It was my cat. I looked after her. I opened the back door and shook the cat food bag a few times. I called to her, 'Rani! Rani! Food! Come on, Rani!' I couldn't see her and shook the bag again. I was about to step out into the back garden when I felt her curling herself around my legs.

After feeding the cat, I went to my bedroom, put my blazer on a coat hanger and hung it on the back of the door. I had just put my dirty clothes in the laundry basket when Rani popped her head round my door. I was about to pick her up when I heard the front door slamming shut. Dad was home.

'You'll have to wait,' I said to Rani, running my hand over her back. She closed her eyes, arched her back, and curled up her tail.

By the time I got to the kitchen, Mum was frying onions in a big pan. Steam from the pan was being sucked noisily into the extractor.

'How many are coming?' I asked. 'Four or five,' she said.

I took some more garlic out of the basket that hung on the wall opposite the window and started peeling.

'Bring my *Kala Kola*,' Dad popped his head into the kitchen and asked me in English, touching his hair. He always spoke to me in English.

'OK, Dad,' I replied, putting a peeled garlic clove in an empty plate Mum had put in front of me. I washed and dried my hands and took a small box of hair dye out of the cupboard. I looked at the box, *Quick-drying Kala Kola.* I took the bottle out, crushed the box in my hand, threw it into a bin and went upstairs to the bathroom.

The door to the bathroom was open. Dad was wiping his face with a towel. Placing the towel in the sink, he held out his hand and I gave him the bottle. He glared back at me and I realised I hadn't opened the bottle for him. I snatched it back, opened the bottle and gave it back to him.

Dad nodded pouring some hair colour into a saucer. Dipping a toothbrush into the saucer he said, 'Too many cars.' 'Yes, Dad,' I said, turning to leave.

'Getting stolen,' Dad went on, dyeing his hair with the toothbrush. 'No one has a proper job round here. When I was young, we went where work was. This lot just want to make quick money.'

'Yes, Dad,' I said.

'And I spend my life phoning the council. Our streetlights don't work. Nothing works round here anymore. I leave a message on a machine and no one bothers to get back to me.'

'Yes, Dad,' I said.

I went back to the kitchen and helped Mum. After the main dishes were cooked, I made some salad and then cleaned up. Rani came in a few times, curled around my leg and went out again.

I cringed when I heard Dad welcoming someone. 'The old farts are here,' I thought.

'What was that?' Mum asked.

'I said nothing, Mum,' I replied.

'Was that your father, I mean?'

'Yes Mum, he was welcoming our guests.'

I washed my hands, placed some orange and apple juice cartons on a tray along with some glasses, adjusted my hijab, and took the drinks into the living room. The room was bursting with grey beards and bloated bellies. I gave my *salaam* to everyone, put the drinks on the table and came out.

'Daughters grow up so quickly,' Dad said as I turned around to leave.

'Such a good girl, your Shamshad, Amjad Saab,' Baba Alam, with his ever-bulging belly said, clearing his throat.

I stopped outside the door and listened.

'Never a bad rumour about her,' the croaky, old voice of Baba Bagha agreed. That's what he always does: agree.

'Amjad Saab, it is official now. Victoria Baths are going to have a Women Only day, and our women will end up going. What a shame on us.'

'Yes!' I whispered, clenching my fist.

'Such a shame,' Baba Bagha added.

'And can you believe it, there are seven days in a week and they chose Friday for Women Only swimming. Friday! They're rubbing salt into our wounds,' Baba Alam complained.

'How could they do it on a Friday?' Baba Bagha asked.

'There was a petition signed by lots of women from East Boarhead,' Dad said in his matter-of-fact voice. 'And some of the women, even the illiterate ones from round here, put their thumbprints on the petition.'

The other old men went silent.

Mum tapped on the side of the pan with her spoon. I rushed back to the kitchen and blurted out, 'There's going to be Women Only swimming in Boarhead, Mum. Isn't that great?'

Mum pursed her lips, shook her head and carried on with the chores.

'Hurry up.' Dad popped into the kitchen.

Mum took the lid off a pan with one hand and stirred the keema, the mince meat, with the other, over and over again. She had a special way of cooking keema. Whilst everyone else added the spice at the beginning and then fried the onions, garlic and ginger, Mum always quickly tossed the meat in a hot wok without any oil until it released its water and began to shine. Only then did she add some hot oil, onions and the other ingredients. There was nothing in the world like Mum's keema.

'Sorry Dad,' I said taking my eyes off Mum.

Mum, stopped stirring the food once Dad had left the kitchen and looked at me in a strange un-Mum-like way. I couldn't tell if she was smirking, smiling or smouldering.

'What?' I asked.

Mum took hold of my hand, pressed it in both of hers and said, 'Nothing.'

I picked up a tray and went to collect the empty glasses. Dad was sitting on his favourite sofa, set into the alcove of a window, dressed as ever in his grey shirt, flowery tie and striped suit. The old men were discussing the same old things, same as ever.

'Amjad Saab, you are a very influential man. There are many Muslims in this town now and, God willing, there will be many more in years to come.'

This was the permanently red-bearded Abdullah Khan from number 127. He was really, really prehistoric and like my Dad, dyed his hair and eyebrows jet black. Mr Khan looked comical as no matter how hard he tried, you could see that the roots of the hair on his head and brows were white. Ever since I could remember, he had driven a taxi for On-time Cars and still drove them now. His sons, like most of the men around here, also drove the taxis or worked in take-aways. Every one of them who came to talk in our house was depressed about not making ends meet.

Mr Khan's favourite subject was that he wanted to get the name of our town changed. For as long as I could remember, he had been going on about it. 'I am always ashamed to tell people I live in this city. I have to say, B.O.A.R.head. I can never pronounce its name, only spell it. How can we name our mosque B.O.A.R head Central Mosque?'

'How can we?' the rest of the old farts agreed.

'One day, *Inshahallah*, one day, God willing,' my Dad replied as he always does when he doesn't know what else he should say.

I went back into the kitchen, placed the empties in the sink and the half-full cartons of juice in the fridge. After wiping the tray, I put some hot kebabs in a serving bowl and placed it on the tray. As I added spoons and side plates, I remembered it was time for prayers.

'Mum, it's getting late for *Isha* prayers.'

She nodded, picking the tray up off the table. I followed her out of the room. She knocked on the front-room door and waited. Dad popped out, took the tray and went back into the room. I went upstairs to do my *wudhu*, to wash myself properly before the prayers. I came out of the bathroom, went into my bedroom and spread the prayer mat on the floor. Rani was curled up on my bed, her tail across her eyes. As I touched the floor with my head, at a moment when I should have only been reciting my prayers, I thought of Karen and laughed.

I got off the mat, brushed Rani off the bed and cursed myself. 'Please forgive me, Almighty, for not concentrating on my prayers,' I implored, and went back and started my prayers again. This time Karen didn't come into my mind. But as soon as I finished, I jumped on my bed, pulled my mobile out of my bag and watched the recording of Karen that I had made that morning. Then it occurred to me!

'Yes, you're going to be famous, Karen,' I said, watching her with her arms by her sides, her face all white with shame. I was going to put her on YouTube as soon as I got near the computer and then send the link to everyone.

Kiran

'Well, Kiran, you really are just dirt,' I thought aloud and walked on. I don't know how long I walked, or in which direction I went. I didn't stop at any road junctions, just crossed. Sometimes cars screeched to a halt, other times they beeped their horns. I just kept going. My ears burnt. My head ached. I felt so cold. My stomach was tight and my throat became dry. I sat down and my breakfast came out all over the pavement. I vomited a few more times and then stood up and walked again.

My mobile rang. It was Mum. I ignored her. My Dad rang. I ignored him.

Mum texted me. I didn't bother opening it and carried on walking. I kept seeing monstrous faces going round and round in front of my eyes. Shamshad laughing, jeering. Holding her mobile phone in front of me.

'Why, Shamshad?' I called out to her. 'What did I do to you?'

Shamshad didn't answer. The monstrous mouths were open, but they were not saying anything. The mobile vibrated in my hand.

A car went swerving past. A red-faced driver, his mouth wide open, saying something to me. But there was only silence.

A cold wind came from somewhere. My head began to throb. It felt as if someone had put a metal clamp on it and was tightening it. Tighter and tighter! I walked on and on.

The clouds thickened above me, but there was no rain.

My hands were wet. My shirt was wet. I felt so hot. I sat down and vomited again.

There were only birds around. I was alone somewhere. And then, out of the silence, I heard Mum's voice. She was calling me. I tried to answer, but my voice was gone. Then I saw her running towards me.

'What are you doing here, you silly girl?' she asked. 'Look at the fool I am, Mum.' I hugged her and cried.

When I stopped crying, I realised I was in the graveyard, sitting under the weeping willow.

'Thank goodness you're alright,' Mum said, wiping my face.

'Love you, Mum,' I said.

She held my hand and we went home. Mum put me to bed.

The first time I woke up, there was a glass of water on the desk near my bed. I was in my nightclothes. The door was open. Mum and Dad were talking downstairs. They were arguing.

Mum screamed, 'It was because of you.' It was a scream I had not heard from her fro a long, long time. I was terrified. *It* would be back in our house.

'It was an accident,' Dad said. 'I wish I gave you a boy.'

'I said I didn't want to,' Mum said, 'didn't I?'

'Let it go, Sharon.'

'You. You. You.'

'I know you wanted a boy, Mum,' I said, lifting my head off the pillow. It was too heavy, I slumped back down.

'Please don't fight over me. I'm sorry for being an accident. Don't fight. Please.'

I forced myself to sit up in bed. I was going to go downstairs and beg them to stop fighting over me. The front door opened and slammed shut. My throat was dry. It hurt. I drank the water and slumped back down again. Behind my closed eyes, open mouths jeered at me. Big, bulging eyes stared at me. Everything was hurled around by a raging wind. The voices, they were the ones that really frightened me. They jeered and asked me so many questions: They wanted a boy, not you. What are you? Who are you? Where are you from? You thought you were white? White? Black? Coloured? Asian? Pakistani? Christian? Muslim? What are you? I kept waking up. I was telling Mum about Shamshad. How she tormented me. How she hated me. Mum just stared back at me. Silently. Sadly.

I heard someone calling my name and woke. Mum was sitting beside my bed. She smiled a *thanksgoodnessyou'realright* kind of smile. Dad was standing in the doorway, one of his lovely, hairy arms dangling by his side, the other behind his back. His loose, white vest rolled over his bulging stomach.

'Nice to have you back,' he smiled, 'Karen, Kiran or Karey? Whoever you are today.'

I sat up in my bed. 'You're really one for words Dad, I thought. 'It's Kiran, Dad,' I said. 'It'll always be Kiran.'

Mum threw a daggerish look at Dad. She kissed me on the forehead and left the room.

'And you really are one,' Dad said, looking at a ray of sunlight coming through the window.

'What?' I leaned up and looked out of the window.

Twigs, leaves and broken branches littered the pavement. Some dustbins were on their sides. Mr and Mrs Mason from next door were surveying the damage from the storm. George was clearing rubbish from his garden, his dog watching him from a short distance.

Dad cleared his throat and said, nodding to the light, 'Kiran. It means a ray of light,' he said.

Suddenly I was filled with rage and cried at him, 'You've taught me nothing, Dad, nothing! I want to be a proper Muslim. Proper something!'

Dad kept quiet. He put one of his feet on top of the other. He was in deep thought.

'Can you teach me, Dad?'

'Yes,' he said. 'I'll teach you...'

Mum came back with a glass of hot milk and gave it to me. I held the glass in both my hands and asked, 'Dad, do you actually know anything about being a Muslim?'

'I do.'

Mum coughed a *pulltheotherone* type of a cough.

'I know a lot more than you think I know,' he said to Mum, but avoided eye contact with her.

'Like fasting?' Mum asked.

Dad curled his big, fat lips, held them up to his nose, and breathed out. '

And praying?' Mum said.

Dad interrupted Mum with a protesting sigh, and said to me, 'I can teach you what you need to know, whenever you are ready.'

I blew into the milk, drank a big mouthful, and then told him, 'I'm ready now, Dad.'

He smiled, and said as he was leaving, 'OK, but get better first.'

I finished off the milk and handed Mum the empty cup. Taking it from me, she said, 'We can discuss it, if you like.'

I nodded-but I wasn't going to let her talk me out of it.

After Mum left, I went back to sleep. It was a deep, deep sleep, without monsters. I woke up in the afternoon. I was feeling sticky but really good with myself. I was going to be a new me. Gone was Karey. Gone was Karen. The WTM were dead. 'Here's to Kiran!' I thought.

I was going to surprise them all. The first thing that Kiran did, which Karen would never have done and Karey wouldn't have thought about, was to change the sheets and pillow cases on her bed. After putting the dirty ones in the wash, I had a shower and went downstairs.

As I was going down, I heard the hiss of a beer can opening. 'Well, it is after 6 p.m.,' I thought.

I checked my mobile. There was a text from Mum: *If you want anything from the shops, ring me on my mobile.*

I went to the kitchen, poured some orange juice into a large glass and walked towards the front room. The door was ajar. Dad was sitting close to the television. The sound was low. I sneaked into the room and peeped at him from behind a large shelf. He was watching an Islam channel. An Imam was giving a talk to some youngsters on the proper way of praying. Dad was puffing away on a cigarette.

Mum, who usually brought the shopping home from Asda on her way back from work, was taking a long time at the shops. I texted her: *Where are you Mum?*

Mum replied almost instantly: *Done in 15 mins. Are you OK?*

Me: *Fine. Dad glued 2 TV.*

Mum: *What's new? Tell him to pick me up.*

As I was about to send my reply to Mum, Dad shouted, 'Kiran, I'm going to pick your Mum up. Text her. Tell her I'll be a bit late.'

He was out of the door before I had a chance to reply.

I sent a text to Mum, *Ur taxi'll b a bit l8. Lol,* and went into the living room.

The room stank of cigarettes and beer, so I opened the windows. A cold wind lapped up the staleness. I sat on the sofa and flicked on the television. The news was on. A helicopter was broadcasting pictures of a mansion surrounded by woods. Breaking News: *Islamic Terror Attack Foiled.* I turned the television off. All of a sudden, I felt exhausted and dozed off. I was in an empty, white room. Without doors. Without windows. 'Karey?' someone called. And then, 'Karen?' And then, 'Kiran?'

I woke up with saliva dribbling from my mouth. Mum and Dad were back and by the time I got off the sofa they had already taken the shopping into the kitchen and Mum was putting it away.

I sleepily walked in, wiping my mouth with a tissue. Mum gave me a great, big, *you'llbealright* kind of a look, and Dad shoved tins into a cupboard. He was in a hurry, and I guessed it was getting nearer to the match. A tin rolled out and fell on his toe. He yelped.

'Serves you right, Lucky,' Mum laughed, looking at Dad who was holding his foot. 'Put them in properly.'

Dad didn't bother saying anything back but took his handkerchief out of his pocket to blow his nose. His weekly lottery ticket fell out, I bent down, picked it up and put it on the table, thinking, 'There's nothing lucky about my Dad.'

Mum picked up the lottery ticket and said, 'Lucky, stop wasting money.'

'You won't say that when I win the jackpot,' Dad said, making a face of exaggerated pain.

'You're the only person I know who has never even won a tenner,' Mum said.

*

Yep. 'There's nothing lucky about my Dad,' I thought again, and asked, 'shall I get you a cold compress, Dad?'

'He needs an ambulance,' Mum said, as Dad put his foot back down and adjusted the tins inside the cupboard, 'don't you, Lucky?'

I suddenly felt really angry with Mum and said, 'His name's not Lucky, is it? It's Liaqat.'

Mum gave me an icy stare. Dad took a deep breath, and said, 'No, Kiran, it's not.'

Mum wiped the kitchen table, went over to the sink, and washed the dishes, which had already been washed – every now and again glancing at me in the reflection in the window.

When she had finished, she looked around the kitchen to make sure everything was where it should be.

'Don't hate me, Mum,' I said. I was determined not to cry. 'But I can't go to church with you anymore. Your Jesus is white. Your Holy Mother is white, and The Father has to be white as well. Look at me! Just look at me!'

Mum whispered, 'It's not like that.'

'I know you hate me,' I said, holding back my tears.

'It's not like that,' Mum repeated, walking up to me.

'You can be what you like, Kiran.' Dad stood up and put his hand on my head.

Mum and Dad exchanged looks that sent shivers down my spine.

I sat down on a chair, put my head in my hands and wept. Mum got me a glass of water. I drank it.

Mum leaned over to an unpacked bag, picked it up and put it on the table. Pushing it towards me, she said, 'Here, I bought these for you.'

Dad picked something out from under a pile of empty bags and hid it behind his back. A big grin ran across his face.

The bag Mum gave me contained a green hijab and a long-sleeved white *kurta* along with some books and a DVD in it. There were small books called *Qaida*s and there was the Holy Quran. There was a book on the Prophet, a book on Islamic history, and a book about fasting. The DVD was called *The Messenger*. I felt so ashamed of myself that I stood up, kissed Mum on the cheeks and hugged her.

'What've you got for her, Lucky?' Mum asked, in a knowing kind of a tone.

Dad walked out of the kitchen backwards, hiding something behind his back. 'Come on, Dad, what you got for me, eh?' I pestered.

'I'll give it to you tomorrow,' he said, trying to get away.

'Let's see it, Dad.'

'Show her, Lucky,' Mum said.

'Liaqat, Mum!'

'He'll always be Lucky to me,' Mum replied.

Dad brought his hand round to the front slowly. He was holding a book as well: *Islam for Dummies.*

We had a really good laugh, and then I said, 'Dad, you can teach me how to pray, can't you?'

'Course I can,' he said, Mum sniggered.

'Can you teach me to read the Quran, Dad?'

'Yep. I read it all, twice, in Pakistan when I was a boy,' Dad said, 'but don't expect me to start believing in all that stuff.'

Mum went silent. Her eyes drifted off for a moment into another world, but then she came back all of a sudden, and said, 'Lucky, go into the living room with Kiran and start teaching her what you know. Let me get the dinner on.'

'I can teach her, you know,' Dad said.

'Go on then,' Mum said.

Dad rubbed his hand on his stomach and then on his head, and replied, 'I will.' Turning to me, he said, 'Come on, Kiran, let's start right now. We'll start with the *Qaida*, and you can learn it just like I did. And then I'll teach you how to pray.'

Mum sniggered again. I went to the living room with Dad carrying the books. He cleared the coffee table and sat on the sofa. I sat down next to him.

'Do you mind if I just check on the score before we start?' Dad asked, holding the TV remote.

I smiled and shook my head. He flicked through a few screens and then turned the television off. He opened the first page of the *Qaida*, pointed to the first letter, and said, '*Alif*.'

'*Alif*,' I repeated.

'*Bey*,' he said, pointing to the next letter.

I repeated as he went along. I was so happy to be sitting with my Dad learning Arabic letters that I must have been the happiest girl in the world. I couldn't remember any other time we had sat together for so long, me and my Dad. As we were going over the letters for a second or third time, Mum came into the room and moaned, 'Lucky! Don't smoke a cigarette next to Kiran, and not while you're trying to teach her to read the Quran!'

Dad quickly stubbed it out, blowing the smoke away from me. 'I think you've done enough for today on the reading,' he said.

'You're going to teach me how to pray?'

'Course I am,' he said, walking out of the room. Mum smiled at me with a sort of *I'dliketoseethat* kind of a look and followed Dad out. I put the *Qaida* away and went to the kitchen to help Mum. That was when I heard Dad stomping down the stairs calling me back into the living room. Mum came with me.

Dad was staring all around the room looking bit puzzled. He said, 'I can't remember which way the *Kabah* is.'

'Mum nodded towards the television corner. Dad looked up at the ceiling for a moment, and said, 'Yes. You're absolutely right.'

'I bet you'd have said that whatever Mum said,' I thought.

'You haven't got a prayer mat,' Mum said.

'I have,' he said, spreading a big, red towel in the space in front of the television. It was a Manchester United towel, with a picture of Alex Ferguson on it.

'I'm not praying on that…'

Dad picked the towel up, turned it over and spread it out on the floor. It had a picture of Wayne Rooney on the other side.

'Oh Dad!'

He stepped onto the towel, raised his hands to his ears, and said, 'First you do this, and you say "*Allah o Akbar*".' Bending down towards his knees, he went on, 'And then you do this and,' he stood upright, 'then you do this…'

Mum interrupted, 'For God's sake, Lucky, you're drinking beer and teaching Kiran how to pray!'

Handing a half-drunk can of beer he was holding in his hand to Mum, he said, 'You're right about that.'

'You'd better take this girl to the mosque or somewhere,' Mum advised. She wants to learn it properly.'

Aren't Mums just full of surprises? I had got myself into a bit of a sulk. I really wanted to dress up but couldn't decide what to do. I was going to ask Mum to help me dress up for the Halloween party at school, but the way she had gone all quiet ever since I told her I wanted to be a Muslim, like *it* was going to hit our house again, made me think it was better not to bother.

'Kiran, sweetheart…?'

'What've I done now?' I grunted, turning my face away from her.

'Haven't you forgotten something?' Mum asked, coming closer to me.

'What?'

'What's tonight, dear?'

'Tonight's, tonight. What is it with you?'

'You're angry, aren't you?'

'No.'

'You *are*,' Mum said, stroking my head.

'Not,' I replied, brushing her hand off. Don't you just hate it when Mums do this?

'It's Halloween, Kiran.'

'So?'

'I thought you wanted to go to your party at school.'

I turned around. She was all smiles. She had a shopping bag in her hand. Putting the bag on my bed she asked, 'What do you want to dress up as?'

I didn't reply. I could hear Dad stomping up the stairs.

'What about a big, hairy monster?' Mum said, pulling a big mask out of the bag; it had long, straggly hair, a hairy face and red vampire teeth.

I burst out laughing. Dad popped his head into my room and then came in. He stared at Mum's hideous thing, running his hand over his big belly.

'What's so funny?' Mum asked. 'It's a Halloween costume.'

Dad started laughing and Mum asked him all serious like, 'What's with you, Lucky?'

'I'm just laughing 'cause she's laughing,' and then turning to me he asked, 'What's the joke, Kiran?'

'It's not a joke, Dad. If I put this thing on at school they'll say I look like you,' I said.

Mum laughed. Dad waved his hand dismissively in the air and went to the bathroom. After he left, I said to Mum, 'Seriously though, Mum, I want to be something special, not just a mask from a shop.'

'Well I won't bother showing you the other one then,' Mum said, shoving the hairy thing back into the bag. 'I got a load of paints. What shall we do?'

I turned my computer on and searched for some ideas. And then I saw one, the perfect one for me. I could just picture myself in it. One side of my face painted in sharp angles of blood red. The other side white, with shining red lipstick, with my messed-up hair falling on my face.

Dad flushed the toilet, came out of the bathroom, popped his head into my room again and said, 'Mum and daughter moment, is it?'

He waited for us to respond but we ignored him and he added, 'Halloween this week, sports week next week. Don't you lot study any more, just party?'

We ignored him again and he went back downstairs.

I pointed to the one I liked and Mum said, 'Perfect.'

She rummaged about in the bag and brought some paints out. I sat on a chair in front of my desk and looked at myself in my big mirror that sat on top of the desk. Mum ran her fingers through my hair saying, 'It's so soft, your curly hair, so soft.'

'I was thinking, Mum, I'd like it all messy - but what do you think of it being spiky?'

'Spiky!' Mum giggled like a little girl. 'Yeh, spiky, really spiky. 'Crikey!' Mum said. 'OK. I got all the stuff for it.' We both laughed.

Mum went downstairs to get a tray so she could squeeze the paint onto it and I went through a few more images of ghouls and things like that. I thought maybe I would look good as a hook-nosed witch, but then rejected the idea with the thought that half the gormless girls at school would turn up as witches with stupid broomsticks. Then there was this Dracula-type with big, bloody fangs, but I didn't like this one either, as half the barmy boys fancied themselves as vampires. By the time Mum came back, I was convinced I had made the wrong choice but then decided I could see what I looked like and if I didn't like it, I'd go for a witch.

Squeezing some red paint onto a stainless-steel tray, Mum said, 'You've always been like this, you know.'

'Like what, Mum, a monster?'

'No, silly! Once you make your mind up, there's no changing it,' Mum said, dipping a brush into the red paint.

'If only,' I thought.

'You know, Kiran, if you have spiky hair, maybe blood-red lightening streaks might be better than splotches.'

'OK,' I said, and thought, 'You're wicked, Mum. Perfect.'

As she drew the first lightning shape on the left side of my face, Mum said, 'Do you remember the mp3 player we bought you for your tenth birthday?'

I smiled. I loved Mum telling me things about when I was younger.

'You'd taken it to school with you and you're not allowed to do that, are you?'

I shook my head. Mum's brush slipped.

'Don't move!' She put the brush down in the tray, picked up a tissue and cleaned my face a little, saying, 'I had to go to school and get it back for you. All the way home in the car, you kept saying, "I didn't know it was in the bag." And, "So and so brings one, and nothing happens to them, and it's so unfair." When we got home, your Dad was snoring on the sofa. I went into the kitchen and you came in after me, with your new headphones plugged into your ears, holding your new toy. The music was so loud I could hear it even as I washed my hands. I could hear your Dad shouting for something. And then he barged into the kitchen. You were so startled you dropped the mp3 player on the floor and it broke.' Mum dipped the brush into some black paint and asked, 'Do you know what you said to your Dad?'

'No!' I lied.

Mum picked up a clean brush and said, swirling it around in the red paint, 'You turned around towards your Dad and shouted, "You broke my mp3 player." He was so shocked, he nearly jumped out of his skin and he said, "You dropped it, not me." And you said, "It's because of you and Mum that I was born, and if I hadn't been born, I wouldn't have dropped it and it wouldn't have broken and I hate you".'

'What did Dad say?' I asked Mum, hoping that this time I might get the bit of this story that never seemed to come out.

Mum went quiet and continued swirling the brush in the red paint. She took a deep breath and said, carefully painting the outline for the teeth on my face, 'He didn't.'

I wanted to say to Mum, 'I know he went quiet, just like you go all quiet,' but instead I let out a false laugh and she continued painting my face.

Mum was about to leave to get some spray for my hair but I stopped her.

Pointing to the mirror I said, 'Mum, this is stupid.'

Dad was coming back up the stairs. Mum nodded towards Dad's footsteps and said, 'He's on the beer again.'

Ignoring her, I said, 'I look ridiculous,' and rushed past her. I wanted to get to the bathroom before Dad went in. He was already at the top of the stairs. He saw me and screamed.

'Dad!' I hissed back, ran into the bathroom and quickly washed everything off.

I came back into my bedroom still drying my face with a towel. Mum and Dad were looking at each other. Mum had her hands on her hips and Dad was scratching his arm.

'I'm not going,' I said.

Mum smiled, opened the bag on the bed and pulled out another mask. It was of Guy Fawkes, his white plastic face and his perfect black eyebrows, with his moustache going up towards his puffed, red cheeks and his sliver of a beard running down his chin from the middle of his bottom lip.

'Mum, you are the best,' I said. It was perfect. I could just put it on and take it off.

'Guy Fawkes, Sharon!' Dad said, rubbing his head with both his hands.

'What's wrong with that?' Mum asked in disbelief at Dad.

'Yeh, what's wrong with that, Dad?' I asked, throwing the towel onto my bed.

Dad ignored me and said to Mum, 'He was a Catholic, Guy Fawkes was.'

'And?' Mum said.

'You're one. Have you no shame, all this burning of the poor Catholic Guy every fifth of November?' Dad looked so serious.

'It's not the fifth of November, if you haven't worked it out,' Mum said. She was having difficulty stopping herself from laughing.

‘He’s the only man who has ever wanted to go to the Houses of Parliament for the right reason,’ Dad said.

Mum burst out laughing. She pushed Dad towards the door saying, ‘You’re outrageous. Outrageous. Just go to the bog, you’ve had too much beer.’

As Dad walked out of my room, I tried to work out what was so funny, but couldn’t and then I understood and shouted after Dad, ‘You are just mad, Dad. Mad.’

As he shut the door of the bathroom Mum called after him, ‘And just so you don’t forget, Kiran is in the 100-metre finals at school next Wednesday. And you’re going to cheer her on. I’m working late.’

I put the mask on my face and said to Mum, ‘He won’t remember.’

‘He’ll be there,’ Mum said as Dad went past.

‘He won’t,’ I argued.

Dad looked at me and said, ‘Oh yes he will. And if you win, he’ll take you on a treat.’

‘You will take her on a treat, even if she doesn’t,’ Mum said. ‘It’s about time you spent some quality time with your daughter, and less with the lager cans.’

‘Bitter,’ Dad corrected Mum.

Mum dropped me off at the school party. The assembly hall looked really spooky. There were dark, painted lanterns all around. Black drapes hanging down the walls. Large candles burned on the stage. The hall was full of Draculas; Spider-Men with fangs; witches and skeletons galore and to my surprise there was only one other Guy Fawkes. This other Guy Fawkes saw me and swaggered towards me followed by four broom-wielding witches.

When he got close to me, I said, ‘Hey, Guy, great minds think alike, eh.’

Guy Fawkes's hands went up, as if in disbelief. The witches looked at each other and giggled.

Just then, Guy Fawkes grabbed a broomstick off one of the witches and prodded me hard in the chest. It hurt.

'How dare you!' he said. It was a voice I knew well and dreaded.

As soon as I heard Shamshad's voice from behind the Guy Fawkes mask, my blood froze. She prodded the broomstick into me again, harder this time. I think it was a Year 8 who stopped me from falling. I hated my mask, but I was glad I was wearing it. It meant Shamshad and her witches wouldn't be able to see my stupid, ugly face. I know I should have said something to her, told her what a bitch she was, but that was me, the good little girl, who never did anything wrong, just always wanted to please everybody.

I moved away from her and her cronies as fast as I could. A Dracula with one of his canine teeth missing said to me as I rushed past him, 'Penny for the Guy.' A Frankenstein laughed. But I found nothing funny. I kept turning around, trying to see if Shamshad was pursuing me. I waited for a little while and when I was sure she was nowhere near the main door, I bolted out of the hall and telephoned Mum to pick me up. I was so relieved when she said she was already in the school car park.

'How was it, dear?' Mum asked as I got into the car.

'Great.'

'Didn't you want to stay longer and have fun?' she said. 'I was happy to sit and read the newspaper - done that for years.'

'Yes, Mum,' I said, as she reversed the car out of the car park.

'I bet there were lots of Guy Fawkes?' Mum said.

'Just one,' I said.

'That's good then, you were unique.'

'No, I meant there was one other.'

'Who was that?'

'Shamshad,' I said coldly.

Mum looked away from me and went quiet. Just as well. I didn't want to talk to her. Besides, even if I did, she was now locked behind her silence. I was free to think about what a mess my life was. What was it with Shamshad? She just never let up putting me down. She could be so bad and still have so many friends, while I was alone, always just being nice. I was good at home, I was good at school and I thought I was good with my gang - but look at me. A laughing stock at school, and at home I never knew what I might say that was so bad that *it* was always lurking in some dark corner.

Sitting next to Mum, I watched the world outside the car flash by like a bad dream. I saw myself at school the next day, at the final, Shamshad's friends cheering for her. She was bigger than me, but clumsy. She always got a better time than me, but then she had everything I didn't.

'Well, Kiran,' I said to myself inside my head, 'stop being like yourself for once; give her a piece of her own game.'

Unlike me, Shamshad had to win and be the best at everything. I didn't care if I didn't win, I don't even know how I made it to the finals, but she always had to be first. A sly smile came across my face as I saw myself running next to her. She'd be really, really focused. I was going to make sure she didn't win. I would wind her up just by being close to her. And then, just as the race started I'd fall and trip her up, and watch her roll on the ground. Perfect thought. And then I thought, no, they would just start the race again, it was only 100 metres. Maybe I could go up to her and say some things that would really upset her. It was easy for me, I just had to open my mouth in her company.

As Mum pulled into our street, I had another idea. Why not beat her fair and square? Well, that is, after winding her up at the beginning.

When we got home, Mum said to Dad, in an icy sort of a way, 'It's Kiran's 100-metre final tomorrow.'

'OK,' Dad said from the living room.

'You don't have to come, Dad, it's fine.'

'OK,' he replied.

I flicked off a shoe; it landed in the middle of the hallway. I flicked the other; it went past the first and hit the kitchen door. Mum, who was halfway up the stairs, glared down at me. I glared back at her. 'No, I'm not going to pick it up, and I don't care what you think. Besides, you're in one of your moods, where you're just going to lock yourself away anyway.'

Mum turned around without saying anything and went up into her bedroom.

As Mum slammed her bedroom door shut, Dad called out, 'Kiran, dear, can you get us a can from the fridge?'

'No,' I shouted back.

'Good girl, make sure you get one of the cold ones from the back,' Dad said.

'Dad!' I hissed under my breath, thinking, 'What planet are you on?' I was halfway up the stairs when I felt really guilty. Dad was just a big softy who didn't know what time of day it was, unless it was a match time. I stopped, turned round and was about to go and get him his beer when I felt a sudden surge of anger. 'No, he can get it himself,' I thought, and carried on upstairs.

Shamshad

Laila and Aisha turned up at the Halloween party as witches. Aisha, with her ridiculously long wobbly nose and rubbery chin, looked a sight. And Leila was wearing a long black burka, all torn into strips that dangled about her.

I didn't see the other Guy Fawkes at first, it was Laila who did. She nudged me in the side and teased, 'Shamshad, look what Jake's turned up as.'

'He's too small and skinny,' I said.

The witches made some sort of spooky noise.

Laila flicked her broomstick at me, reciting some things by way of a spell. The broom bit of her broomstick was just a bit of cardboard cut-out that had been hurriedly painted and sellotaped to a stick. It broke off and poked her in the eye. She yelped. We laughed. I laughed all the more at the way she was dressed in her stupid little witch outfit. The only thing witchy about it was the black cloak; she could easily have passed for a fairy, with a bit of red paint on her face.

At first, when Laila pointed Guy Fawkes out to me, I was dead chuffed; at least I wasn't the only one. But when this Guy said in Karen's voice, 'Hey Guy, great minds think alike, eh,' I just flipped and prodded her as hard as I could. If it hadn't been for the stupid, red-headed, hairy monster of a clown behind her, she would have fallen flat on her backside.

I was about to give her a piece of my mind when Laila tugged my arm and said, 'Let up, girl, not worth it.'

As always, she was right. Me and my anger, we were never so bad until Karen came onto the scene. I took a deep breath, went up to Karen and said in her ears, 'You pathetic copycat.'

If she didn't have her mask on, I would have been able to see her dirty little face for what it was, a no good, dirty little half-breed face.

When she got her balance back, she turned away from me and walked off into the party.

After Karen left, Laila said, 'You know she's in the 100 metre finals.'

'No,' I lied. Of course I knew. Everyone knew, and ever since she had got into the same final as me, I had been running twice a day, just to make sure I beat her.

'There's your chance to get one over on her in front of the whole school,' Aisha Sadiq said, holding her stick in one hand and the broom head in the other.

'She always wants to be the best,' one of the witches next to Laila said.

'Yeh, Laila, why don't you put another spell on her,' I said.

'What, with a broken broom?' she replied.

The others laughed and I joined in. I was scouring the party, trying to see where Karen had disappeared to. Though I didn't see Karen leaving, one of my witches said Guy Fawkes ran out of the hall. Then she added, with her broomstick between her legs, her bum wiggling about, 'Like it was bonfire night.' It was such a laugh.

I got to school well early for the races, tied my hair up tightly in a thin, white cloth, got into my black leggings and a black and golden top, put on my trainers and warmed up in the changing rooms. I was still warming up when Laila and my gang came in. We did a few high fives and I went out into the fields. As I was walking out of the main entrance, I saw such a pathetic sight: Karen and her Dad, Lucky, coming towards me. They were late. Karen walked fast. Her Dad was panting behind her. He stopped a short distance away from the gate. Karen came straight towards me, bumped into me and said, 'Get out of my way, you fat cow.'

I was stunned. Before I could say anything else, she was gone. My gang looked at me in disbelief.

'That's it,' I said, clenching my fist. I turned around and was about to go for Karen when the bald-headed Mr Armstrong, our P.E. teacher, came out. He was wearing his normal blue sports suit with white stripes. He had a stopwatch dangling in front of his chest.

'Come on girls, why are you hanging about here?' he said, walking past.

Then he stopped, did a little jog on the spot, cracked his neck and added, 'And you need to get warmed up, Shamshad.'

'Yes, sir,' I said, still reeling from what Karen had just done.

'And good luck,' he told me, walking away, moving his shoulders up and down.

Karen's Dad followed Mr Armstrong to the parents' and teachers' section of the playing fields.

Laila held my hand, saying, 'Come on.'

Walking to the fields, I chewed my teeth and promised myself that I would get Karen for what she had just done.

Everyone who was in the final had a parent or two at school. Walking away from my friends, how I wished mine would come to something at school, just once. I shook my head, trying to chase this silly thought away. Dad would never come, he never had the time and Mum didn't even know where my school was.

Karen came out and ran to her Dad, gave him a hug and came towards us in the line-up. She smiled at the other kids in the final then walked straight up to me and said, 'Your leggings are sticking up your big, fat arse.' She looked me straight in the eye, nodded to my chest and added, 'And you should have worn something looser, you show-off.'

Blood rushed to my ears. 'Oh Allah, stop me from flattening her right here,' I thought. I looked to see if anyone else had heard what she said. No one else was close by. Laila waved at me. I turned around and Karen was in her place at the starting line, next to me, swinging her arms about.

'Wait till this is over,' I hissed at her. She looked at me and tapped her behind.

'Finalists, get ready,' Mr Armstrong's voice boomed out of the loudspeakers.

The kids let out a roar. I took a deep breath and tried to forget Karen. Then the starting gun went off. Just as we set off the gun sounded again. A false start. A teacher went up to Karen and gave her a warning.

After a few moments, Mr Armstrong's voice boomed out again, 'Finalists ready.'

'Go on, Karen,' I thought. 'Do it again.'

Just then, the gun went and we were off. Karen was away so fast, but I quickly caught up with her. We were all neck and neck at first. I remembered Mr Armstrong's words, 'Hold yourself together for the first 20 metres and then let go.' I was blind to the others in the race. I could see Karen giving it all she had. She was a little in front of me. And then I blotted her out of my mind. I blotted everything out of my mind. I was going to win this.

Twenty metres went by in a flash. Karen was a bit further ahead of me by then, but I gave it all I had and caught up with her. As I went past I saw her in the corner of my eyes, panting madly. I pushed on and on. She kept catching up. I heard someone cheering me on, and pushed myself even harder. Karen was a hair's breadth behind.

I saw the finishing line. Mr Armstrong was there, slightly bent forward, holding the stopwatch in his hand. There were two other teachers with stopwatches. I ran and ran and ran as fast as I could and crossed the line. I raised my hands to the Almighty for granting me my wish.

I looked for Karen. She was on her back, on the track, not far from me. I waved at Laila. My gang were jumping up and down with joy. Mr Armstrong wrote something down on his scorecard and conferred with the other teachers, nodded, pulled a cordless microphone out of his pocket and tapped on it, saying, 'What an absolutely amazing race that was.' He paused, waved his hand towards the kids and added, 'Don't you all agree?'

A deafening cheer went up.

'And I am pleased to announce,' Mr Armstrong continued when the noise went down, 'in the third place, Jonathan West at 12.35, in the second, Susanne Williams.' He paused again.

'You piece of trash,' I cursed Karen. 'Didn't make it, did you?'

She turned away from me. Mr Armstrong continued, 'Shamshad Khan, 11.29, what an absolutely amazing result. One of the best ever.' The Head, who was standing close by Mr Armstrong, tapped him on the shoulder. He turned to her and the two of them looked through a piece of paper. Mr Armstrong's face lit up and he announced: 'I've just been told that this is our new school record for the girls' 100 metres.' A deafening roar went up. He waited for the noise to go down and said, 'And Kiran Malik, 11.29, congratulations to the joint winners.'

'Surely I've misheard,' I thought,. 'It can't be.' I looked up into the sky. A big, rolling white cloud was merging into a collapsing face. Just then, I became enraged. I didn't care that everyone was watching. I clenched my fist and went for Karen.

Kiran

I was flat on my back looking up at a big, white twisting and turning cloud, sinking into a sad face. From the corner of my eye, I saw Shamshad come towards me, grunting. I got up quickly and went towards Mr Armstrong. Dad was already there. He was out of breath. He hugged me and said, 'Well done, Kiran, you came second. Well done.' Overhearing Dad, Mr Armstrong said, 'No, Mr Malik, she didn't.'

'Well done anyway, Kiran,' Dad said.

'She came first, along with Shamshad Khan,' Mr Armstrong informed him, going back back towards the starting line, where the next race was lining up.

Dad went silent.

I looked around to see where Shamshad was. I didn't want to meet her in the changing rooms. She was on the other side of the track, surrounded by her cronies.

'I don't feel well, Dad, can I go home now, please?' I said. He looked right through me.

'Dad!' I said more loudly, I don't feel well, I want to go home.' He nodded.

'Can you please come with me to reception, and tell them?'

I looked around once again at Shamshad. She was staring at me. She said something to her mates and I knew she was coming for me. I knew she was coming for me.

'Dad, please hurry up,' I said, walking back to school.

He quickened his pace. I ran past reception, bolted to the changing rooms, grabbed my clothes and rushed back. Shamshad was already in the hallway. Dad was talking to the receptionist.

As I went past Shamshad, she hissed, 'Just wait and see.'

Dad had snapped out of wherever he'd gone and said, walking out of the reception, 'It doesn't matter. I'm still proud of you.'

I didn't reply. I was stung by the word 'still'. *Still,* I thought, you mean because I came joint first or because I came joint first with Shamshad.

Getting into the car, Dad said, 'And on Saturday, me and you are going out to celebrate, just the two of us.'

I threw my stuff on the back seat and sat in the back of the car. 'D and D,' Dad chuckled. 'Daughter and Dad.'

'Oh, yeh,' I thought to myself, 'D and D, that's a new one. As if you'll remember this on a match day.'

On the way home, I thought about the look on Shamshad's face when I said what I did to her before the start of the race. It was worth everything she was going to do to me. At last, for once, me, Little Miss Goody Two-Shoes, me, the little doormat, had slapped her in the face. Dad said something about what I wanted to do on Saturday. I ignored him. He started humming a Pakistani song. I was rummaging about in my bag looking for my mobile. I had a text from Mum: *How did you do?*

I texted her back: *Ask Dad.*

A moment or so later, Dad's mobile buzzed. He got a text. Still humming, he looked at his mobile and stopped humming.

*

I was thinking about D and D when I got home. Dad had never said anything like that before. I tried to work out why he'd said it. It wasn't just Dad, but Mum had also been different towards me ever since I'd said I wanted to be a Muslim. It certainly wasn't because of the race. Maybe they were trying to get me back on track, whatever that was. And the way Mum had sat with me, for Halloween, the way she'd stroked my hair and spoken, it wasn't like her usual, 'Yes dear, fine dear, love you dear, blah, blah, blah.' No, for once I really felt she was there, for me, with me, just for me. And now, I had a special Saturday coming up with Dad…

I was taking a bag of rubbish out when Mum got back from work, but she didn't say anything to me. No hug. No, 'Hello, I'm back!' No 'Well done.' Nothing. She went straight into the living room, and yes, Dad was up to his usual, glued to the telly, beer in hand. She turned the television off. Dad didn't protest. They looked at each other, in a strange sort of way. Mum saw me standing by the door, walked past Dad and shut the door.

I did what I do, when *it* takes over our house and ran to my bedroom, jumped on the bed and said aloud, 'Well, Saturday, you're just a hoax.'

But Saturday did come. And before it came, Mum and Dad talked to each other, in heavy, sad voices. Waiting for Saturday, I tried to catch their words, but they were just words, everyday words, about shopping, and work and just normal everyday chores, but wrapped in something dark, something unmentionable.

Saturday did come and by the time it came, *it* was gone. And on this Saturday, Mum came and woke me up with a kiss. And this Saturday, Mum was wearing a beautiful dress. At first, I thought I was waking up in a dream, but then I heard Dad calling me, 'Breakfast ready in five.'

I looked at Mum. She looked at me. I touched my ear, waiting for the smoke alarm to go off. Me and my Mum burst out laughing.

And this Saturday brought a beautiful, sunny, blue sky. And Dad didn't watch the match. I floated about during the morning trying to work out the big secret that Dad had lined up for me.

All throughout the breakfast of burnt toast and greasy eggs, I kept trying to guess my surprise. Monday was a Bank Holiday and then we had a teacher-training day on Tuesday, so maybe D and D meant Dad was going to take me away on holiday, and if this was the case, we were off to Italy, I reckoned. After Man U, Dad loved A.C. Milan. Or maybe we would go to Bodrum, in Turkey. Dad's mates always went there. He often talked about going there, sitting on a beach, getting a boat and going out into the sea, fishing. Or maybe, just maybe, he would take me into town and get me a new laptop.

Finally, we finished our breakfast and Dad said to me, 'I'm taking you somewhere really special.'

'Where?' I asked.

'Dad and his lovely daughter are going for a boat ride…'

'Boat ride!' I said. I was filled with pride for having guessed that he was going to take me to Turkey.

'We are going rowing. I've booked a boat in Boarhead Park.' 'Boarhead Park. Rowing,' I thought and said, 'Great, Dad.'

And a-rowing we went, Dad and me, in the lake in the middle of Boarhead Park. I sat stiffly in the back of our car, while Dad went on about how wonderful it was for the two of us to spend time together, just me and him.

At one end of the lake, there is a small café and next to this is the office for hiring boats. Dad bought me an ice-cream and whilst I sat there stabbing it with a small white plastic spoon he went off to sort out the boat. There are two islands in the middle of the 's' shaped lake, one in each of the curves of the 's', where ducks and geese and other birds breed. Along the banks of the lake there are big oak trees, some bent towards the lake, others so big and tall their shadows fall across the waters like large monsters, moving over the ripples from the oars of passing boats and the swimming ducks and geese.

By the time Dad came out, my ice-cream had been reduced to a gooey mess.

'Ready?' Dad asked. I nodded.

'Like the ice-cream?'

'Yeh, Dad.'

He went so confidently towards the boat, like he had been rowing all his life, and stepped into the boat with such force that it almost capsized. A boat assistant ran up and held the boat whilst Dad got his balance back.

The boat had two places to sit. One next to the oars and the other in front of that. I sat in front of Dad. The oars were placed on either side of the boat. Dad picked them up, put them into the metal holders and rowed. As he did this, he stood up, took some keys out of his back pocket and sat down again. The boat shook from side to side.

'Careful, Dad.' I laughed. 'Mum says you swim like a brick.'

'Less of that!' Dad said rowing. There'll be no need for that.'

I was surprised. He was so good at rowing! He used both oars together as we pulled out and then used one to turn and the other to move forward and make sure we missed another boat, full of loud-mouthed teenage boys, which was coming at us with full speed. As we went into one of the turns, Dad's rowing became smooth and methodical, the oars going into the water, pushing the boat through it, coming out, dripping, and dropping back again, sounding almost musical.

'He's not such a clumsy oaf, your Dad,' I thought, looking at his big smile on his big, beautiful, fat face. His big, beautiful belly was popping out of his shirt as some of the buttons had become undone. He closed his eyes for a moment and started singing in his own language, a song I had heard him hum many times but never heard him sing.

I wished I could understand, but even without this, it felt so good, listening to him singing.

'What does it mean, Dad?'

He smiled and said, 'Do you remember when I went to Pakistan, when my friend Aziz died.'

I tried to think. I remembered him going, but not much more than that. I put my hands between my knees and nodded.

'I went to the same school as him when I was young. We were like brothers, we were. He was a poor man, who worked in the hills behind my village, for a stone contractor. He used to load trucks with rocks. One day, when he was loading a truck, there was a landslide and he was crushed to death.'

Dad went silent like he was back there. Letting out a deep sigh, he continued, 'It took them two days to move the rocks and get his body out. I arrived in Pakistan as his body was brought to his house and helped to give him his final *ghusal*, his final wash. When the time came to carry him to the graveyard for his funeral, his wife came and insisted on helping to lift his body out of her house. That stupid old Imam Butta said women weren't allowed to do this, but she ignored him. I let her hold her husband's bed and she helped to lift it up and placed it on my shoulder. She started walking with the men and Imam Butta told her to stop. Women weren't allowed to do this. She ignored him again and walked with us. I thought she would stop where the other women stop, just where the last house of the village is and then they come and stand outside the graveyard until the men finish reading the funeral. But she didn't stop. She kept walking. When everyone recited religious chants, she kept quiet. Not crying. But silent. Along the way a woman tried to hold her hand to stop her going, but she snatched it free and kept on walking with us.

'Just as we got past the last house, she sang in a voice so loud and so clear it tore right through me.'

Dad looked at me with sad, sad eyes and sang: *'Baghe ander hik bulbul alarnaan paee see banandhi Ajay na charya toor Mohammed, ud gaee ay kurlandhi.'*

My Dad sang these lines so beautifully, in a voice I didn't recognise, a voice that came out from some depth within him, a place where he didn't go very often.

Before I could ask him what it meant, he translated: 'A nightingale was building her nest in the garden, Oh

Mohammed, it had yet to be finished and she flew away screaming.'

Dad looked behind and rowed away from some branches that were hanging into the lake. Pulling out into a sunny bit of the lake, he looked at me and said, 'I love you, Kiran.'

'Love you too, Dad. Now can you sing it again?' He did.

And then I asked him to sing it again and he did.

I hadn't noticed we had come full circle round of the lake and were going round again.

As we went past the first curve, I saw Shamshad standing close to the bank, near some bushes. She bent down, picked something up and held her hand out as though to lob it at us. Just then I saw a startled bird fly, screaming out of a tree above her.

Shamshad

On the way back home from the park, each time I saw a bird, I thought I saw the one that had screamed out from above me, and each time I heard it, it was as though it was the first time I'd heard it. Had I not heard such a frightful cry of a bird above me, a cry that cut deep into me, I would've lobbed the stone at Karen.

That night I kept falling in and out of sleep, waking up all sweaty. In my dreams, I kept seeing a thick, rolling cloud, changing into faces - mocking faces, faces I should know, but to which I could put no name.

After clicking on my bedside lamp, I opened the bottom drawer of my chest of drawers, carefully so as not to wake anyone else. It is a deep drawer, with a hidden section, which I made myself by placing a bit of matching plywood at the bottom. In this, I keep my secret, secret things, especially my drawings.

On a blank A4 piece of paper, I sketched the outer lines of the cloud.

The lines got thicker and deeper, as though my hand had a mind of its own. A face began to form, a disfigured, horrible face, with accusing eyes, fiery eyes, sorrowful eyes and then just a dark smudge.

I felt cleansed after I finished this drawing. I took out my notebooks from the bottom drawer, lifted the plywood false bottom, placed the drawing on top of the others and went back to sleep: a deep, peaceful sleep.

I woke up late the next morning, glad I wasn't going to see *her* ugly face for a few days. I didn't know she would end up taking my best friend from me.

Our central mosque is in the middle of Boarhead East, surrounded by boarded-up mills and pubs that have long since closed, their yards full of discarded furniture and rusty fridges. Our mosque used to be a church. *Alhamdulillah*, praise be to God, it is a mosque now. To get inside, you have to climb many old steps and walk in through tall, wooden doors. A balcony runs around the main hall. On the sides of the balcony are smaller rooms in which we have lessons. There is a smaller hall for women at the back of the main hall.

It was a bright, sunny day and I went to the mosque early to help clean up after Friday prayers. Laila was with me. She didn't usually come here on Fridays. She went somewhere else, a small place near the college where Muslim students prayed and discussed things. We were waiting for the caretaker to come and open up the study rooms, so we sat on a bench on the balcony, looking out as the mosque began to fill up. It was the wrong time of month for me and Laila, so we weren't going to pray anyway.

I didn't notice her at first. She was sitting on her own not far from us. Her face was turned away, so I couldn't tell who it was. There was something oddly familiar about her. The strange thing was that she was wearing the same green-coloured hijab as me and a long-sleeved, white shirt, exactly the same as mine; even her black trousers were the same as mine.

I prodded Laila and nodded towards her. Laila shrugged her shoulders. I coughed loudly, hoping to get *her* to turn this way, but she sat stiffly, looking down into the main prayer hall. I coughed again. This time loudly. A few men looked up at me from the hall. I pulled back out of their sight.

'Stop it,' Laila whispered.

The girl didn't move. I stood up.

'What you doing?' Laila asked.

I gestured for her to follow me. I took a few steps towards the girl, who took her hands off the balcony and pressed them together.

'It's her,' I whispered to Laila. 'Karen the flashing *hijaban*.'

Laila didn't reply. I sat down next to Karen. Laila sat next to me.

I pressed my elbow into Karen's ribs and asked her, 'What's it with you, Karen? What do you want from us?'

'Please, Shamshad, I just want to start again and be friends,' she said.

'You don't belong here,' I said. Even the sound of her voice made me go into a rage. 'And what's with you dressing up like, eh?'

'I wasn't, I swear, I wasn't…'

Laila interrupted, 'Leave her alone, Shami.' Turning to me, Laila said, 'Everyone is welcome in the house of Allah.'

'I'm with my Dad, and I am going to come here and I'm going to learn - and my name is Kiran,' Karen said.

Just then the prayers started. It was just as well. I was so vexed with Karen, or Kiran, as she wants to call herself for now, I could have smacked her right there. What did she think religion was? A fashion item! You are Karen one day and Kiran the next? You sneer at us, call us scarfies one day, and become one the next? You go to church one day, claiming God had a son, and the next you come here and you can say, 'No, God was not a man, he had no son.' You hang around with your big, ugly gang and they rip our hijabs off our heads, but now you come here all innocent, like?

I looked down into the hall and recognised her father. He came to our street once a week, every Thursday without fail. He was called Lucky Saab on our street. He was in the fourth row down from the front, towards my end of the balcony. It was hard not to miss him, with his long arms and his big stomach. He was doing his *sajda*, touching the floor with his forehead. His shirt had rolled out of his trousers, exposing his builder's bottom. Like daughter, like father, I thought. Shameless! As Mr Lucky Saab raised his head out of the *sajda,* he touched the side of his trouser leg and then raised his fist in the air, looked around, then quickly went down into the *sajda* again with the rest of the line.

'How dare your father do this in the mosque,' I hissed into Karen's ear. 'Disgusting, all of you!'

Karen didn't answer. As the prayers were about to finish, Laila and I left.

The room in which we read the Quran has long, stained-glass windows that curve around the side of the building. We squat on the floor beneath the windows, leaning against the wall, with the Holy Quran in front of us. Girls and children sit in this room. Older boys read next door, in another room like this. I have read the Holy Quran three times and I am on my way to memorising the third *spirah.* *Insha'Allah*, god willing, I am going to learn the holy book by heart.

Once a week I teach younger children how to read the Holy Quran. Laila had gone to the bathroom and I was laying out stands for the children's *Qaida*s when my Dad came in and said to me, 'Someone new is joining today.'

I looked up and put my hand to my mouth. I just managed to stop a squeal turning into a loud '*OMG.*' Karen was standing next to him. Dad looked at me accusingly. I wanted to tell him, 'Dad, she's not my friend. I hate her. I had nothing to do with her coming here.' He adjusted the white lace prayer cap on his head and left, tapping the small cane in his hand which he always carried in class.

I looked at Karen and thought, 'You're not getting away with whatever you're up to - I'll get you!' She turned her face away from me, looked up at the windows, then down towards the row of stands, and then towards the storeroom in the corner. She had the same headscarf on as she did when she came to school in her miniskirt, but today she was wearing a white full-sleeved top with loose-fitting black trousers.

Laila came back, and I said to her, 'Look what the cat brought in.'

'Hi, Karen,' Laila said, stepping into the room past her.

Karen nodded, and said, 'It's Kiran.' She locked her hands in front of her and tapped her right foot.

Laila smiled, tapped her own head, and said a bit louder, 'Hi, Kiran.'

I was upset with Laila for putting me down in front of Karen, and said, 'You will always be Karen to me.'

I wanted to smack Karen right there, on her nose, and throw her out of the mosque.

'Where do you think you are, in a disco?' I said to her, pointing towards her foot.

She looked down at the ground and carried on tapping her right foot. 'Come on in, Kiran…'

I gave Laila such a stiff stare she stopped mid-sentence, but then she looked away from me and said, 'I'll teach you today.'

'You've only been here a minute, Karen,' I thought, 'and you've already taken my friend from me.'

'It's my class and *I'll* teach her,' I said to Laila. Turning to Karen, I pointed to the far side of the room, and said, 'Over there, with the babies.'

As Karen went over to where I had told her to sit, the children came running noisily up the stairs and went to their places. Laila placed a *siparah* in front of her, and Karen sat down and crossed her legs. 'Start your *sabaq*, your lesson,' I said to the class, and the room burst into the beautiful sound of Arabic from the mouths of the children.

'Keep still, Karen!' I said, sitting down in front of her.

She looked round the room, but didn't say anything back to me. 'Open the *Qaida*,' I said.

She did, and before I had given her the first lesson, she started reading, '*Alif zabr Aa - Alif Zair Ae; Bey zabr Ba...*'

'Stop! Stop! Stop!' I shouted.

Everyone in the room went silent. Some of the children giggled. Turning to the kids, I asked, 'Who told you lot to stop?'

They burst into rhythmic recitations again. Seeing my Dad standing at the door, the children increased their volume.

Pointing to the letters in front of Karen, I said to her, 'That's not proper, *Karen*. It's *Aa, Ba...*'

'That's not how my Dad taught me,' Karen said.

'What's that rubbish collector know?' I whispered to her. 'He's just trash.'

'Don't insult my Dad,' Karen said, grinding her teeth.

'Trash! Trash! Trash!' I taunted.

My Dad came up to us. I moved back a little. He held the cane in his hand behind his back. He asked, 'How's Lucky Saab's daughter getting on in her first *sabaq*?'

'She refuses to learn the proper way to pronounce the Arabic letters,' I said.

'Pindu villagers,' Dad murmured to himself. 'And England did nothing for them.

'That's how my Dad taught me, sir,' Karen whimpered.

'Imam Lucky Saab did, did he?' Dad laughed.

'Dad, you're proper brilliant,' I thought.

The children lowered their voices. Dad looked around the room and they started reciting loudly again.

'My granddad once taught me like this,' Karen said.

'Yes,' I thought to myself, clenching my fist, 'go on, say more, *Karen*.'

Dad brought the cane out into his right hand. The children recited even louder. 'Go on, Dad,' I thought, 'smack her one.'

Dad pushed the cane towards Karen's chest. He moved the cane around her chest and slowly took it up to her chin, forcing her to raise her head. He said, 'I know that *kafir* very well...'

I caught a glimpse of Laila. With her hand in front of her mouth, she was staring at Dad, shaking her head.

'Don't you call my granddad a *kafir*!' Karen shouted and jumped up. She was crying.

The children stopped. Dad stepped back from her. She lowered her head and ran out of the room. Laila went after her.

Kiran

Laila walked out with me. We went quickly down the bare wooden stairs, the noise of the children reciting their lessons fading slowly away, into the echoes of our feet. I felt so angry with myself for going to the mosque and for not pushing the cane away. It made me feel dirty inside.

It felt as if the walls of the mosque were caving in on me. Someone laughed somewhere. It bounced around me. When Laila tried to hold my hand, I snatched it away.

'It was disgusting what he did with the cane,' Laila said, 'disgusting.'

I cringed. A shiver ran down my spine.

'I'm alright, you know,' I told her, barging out of the doors of the mosque. Stepping into a gusty wind, I said, 'You don't have to come with me.' Patchy, dark clouds were blotting out the sun. There was a slight chill in the air.

'You're so brave, you know, and I never did thank you for standing up for me the other day.'

'I didn't,' I said, 'I just hate Donna.'

Laila pressed on my hand, and we walked on. Dad was leaning against the wall at the bottom of the steps, glued to his mobile, oblivious to the litter flying around him. Clenching his fist, smiling and frowning in turn. He wore an earphone, which was plugged into the mobile.

When I got close to him, I pulled the earphone out of the mobile. He was listening to a football match commentary. He looked at me in disbelief. His unshaven face twitched. It was like seeing the face of a little boy who'd had his candy snatched from him.

Laila looked at me and we burst out laughing.

'What's so funny?' Dad asked.

'It's a girly thing, Uncle,' Laila said.

We laughed more. And then I gave Laila a big hug and burst into tears.

'What's the matter, Kiran?' Dad asked.

Getting myself together, I pulled away from Laila, wiped my face with the corner of the hijab and replied, 'Like Laila said, Dad.'

We burst out laughing again. Dad plugged his earphone back in. A moment or so later he pulled it out and threw it on the ground, then bent down, picked it up and put it in his pocket, saying, 'I can't believe it. I just can't.'

'He always says this when Man U lose,' I whispered into Laila's ears. 'Now he's going to clench his fist and say exactly the same thing again.'

He did.

When he calmed down, I pointed back to the mosque, and asked, 'What were you doing in there, Dad?'

'Praying, of course.'

'What was about, with the fist?'

He leaned closer to us, lowered his voice, shrugged his shoulders like a child, and said, 'I'd set the mobile to receive a message when Man U scored. How was I to know we would lose 6–1 to City? I can't believe it, I just can't!'

'Dad, you're terrible!' I said.

'I didn't mean to raise my fist.' Dad blushed. Well, the closest to blushing I have ever seen him. 'I felt really silly when everyone else went into *sajda.*'

'Didn't anyone say anything to you, Dad?'

'When praying, we are meant to be so deep in prayer, we're supposed to forget about the world around us,' Laila answered.

Dad nodded, sheepishly.

'Your builder's bottom was showing, Dad.'

'Maybe Uncle, you could get braces like some of the old men,' Laila said, with a giggle.

'Hey, less of the *old*, young lady!' Dad said, pushing himself off the step.

'I'm not coming back here again, Dad,' I told him.

'You mean the Almighty got a free prayer out of me?' Dad smirked.

'Uncle, you're unbelievable!' Laila said. Just then, the sun came out.

Laila put her arms around me and said, 'You can come with me and learn.'

'Dad, you go home and I'll stay with Laila for a bit.'

Dad was clearly relieved. He put his hand in his pocket, pulled out a five-pound note and said, handing it to me, 'Don't be late.'

'I won't,' I promised.

As he turned around to leave, Laila said, 'You can come along to the lessons as well, Uncle.'

He waved his hand dismissively in the air and walked on.

We crossed the road and as we stepped onto the pavement opposite, Laila pulled her headscarf off. She had shoulder-length, sharply cut hair. A green ribbon was tied across her forehead. Her star-shaped, silver earrings flickered in the bright sunlight.

'What are you doing?' I asked.

Folding the headscarf into a small ball, she said, 'Sometimes I feel like being covered, sometimes I don't. Right now I don't.' She put the headscarf into her pocket, and said, 'You can take yours off if you like.'

'No, I feel better with it on,' I said.

'I know what you mean,' Laila said. After looking round to see if anyone was watching, she adjusted her bra, and said, 'Sometimes when I wear my hijab, I make them stick out.'

Pointing to my chest, I laughed, 'Not much I can do with these.'

'Men can't keep their eyes off women in hijabs,' Laila said, 'especially *goray*, you know.'

We stopped talking as a Boarhead Operational Services road-cleaning van went past us, its brushes sweeping up everything from the sides of the road. When its noise faded, I told Laila how, when I'd been little, Dad told me he worked for the local council. I was so proud of him. I thought he had the most important job in the world. He told me he worked for Operational Services, which made sure that everything was kept clean so that there were no diseases like the plague. Then when he got promoted, he told me he was now like a pilot of a plane. When I got older, I realised that he was really a dustbin man. And now he drives the big collection truck. And he loves being called Lucky. Laila and I laughed and laughed till our sides ached.

'I feel like you're me best friend,' I said after we got our breath back, 'and I hardly know you.'

'Me Mum and Dad got married and hadn't seen each before that,' Laila said.

We broke into yet more laughter. When we stopped again, Laila sucked her teeth and said, 'Shamshad told me she hates you 'cause she says you're half-caste.

'Did she really say "half-caste"?'

'And she hates you for leaving Islam…'

'But I am trying now, aren't I, Laila?'

'She's just a messed-up kid. But tell me, what's it with your family and Shamshad's?'

I thought about it and tried to work it out so it would make sense. 'I don't know where to start.'

'Just say it,' Laila urged.

I took a deep breath and said, 'My Dad's family and her Dad's family hate each other.'

'Well, who doesn't know that,' Laila said. 'I heard your Dad and her Dad were once best mates.'

'I heard that too, but it's one of those things we don't talk about at home. You know how Mums and Dads can be when they don't want you to talk about something…'

'I know what you mean. In my house, Laila interrupted, 'if we're watching telly and someone kisses on the screen, everyone looks away and the men start talking about cars and the women about cooking. And as soon as the kissing stops, they start watching again and pretend as though nothing happened.'

'Seriously though,' I continued, 'I don't really know what happened between our families, but I think someone from their side in Pakistan fancied someone from our side. Their someone got engaged to someone from our side against everyone's wishes, and our someone charged in on the wedding night and took away their someone. There was a shootout, like, and people got killed.'

'Oh my god,' Laila said.

'It gets worse,' I went on. 'You know Shamshad's lot have a lot of their clan here.'

Laila nodded.

'Well, that wedding thing happened yonks ago...'

Laila butted in with, 'But here's here and there's there, and it was a long time back so what's it with all the aggro' between your families now?'

'Well, things never let up back over there, and a few years ago, I'm not sure exactly what happened but someone from Shamshad's side there and three of her cousins from here went and killed someone from our side.'

'It was on the news here, wasn't it!' Laila exclaimed. 'I didn't know it was your lot.'

'So now you know why she hates me, then,' I said. 'Bet your lot aren't as bad as ours.'

'Our lot, if they have a big meal together, can't digest it without a good scrap afterwards,' Laila said.

'But they don't kill a few people...'

'If something like this happened back there, in our part, they wouldn't kill a few people like your lot.' Laila paused and then said: 'They'd wipe the whole tribe out.'

We both laughed and laughed like we'd lost it. When we finally stopped, I said, 'But then I heard another story, Laila. You see they own a lot of land in the village and we worked for them. When my granddad or my great-granddad refused to work for them, their side came and took some girls from our side and someone got killed, maybe at a wedding...'

'When did all this happen?' Laila asked.

'About a zillion years ago,' I said, and we laughed a bit more.

Then Laila wanted to know: 'Have you ever asked your Dad what really happened?'

'I did once or twice, but he said what he usually does.' I did the best impersonation of Dad that I could manage: '"It's all water under the bridge".'

'You know, Kiran,' Laila said, flicking her hand in the air. 'None of it truly matters.'

'What doesn't?' I was trying to find a way of saying something I really, really wanted to tell Laila.

'All this stuff. I mean, what does it really matter?'

'No, there's something else you don't know, Laila.'

'What is it? Tell me.'

'I don't know how to tell you.'

'We're mates, you can tell me anything,' Laila said, placing her hand on mine.

'It's not that I want to keep a secret from you,' I said. 'There's something else between us and them, I mean between my family and Shamshad's. You know when old folk talk, well, you know how they all gossip about each other.'

Laila let out a *don'tIknowit* sort of a laugh.

'But if I am ever around and someone mentions Shamshad's family, a strange frightening silence comes into the room. They all go quiet and don't look at each other. It's like there's something they really don't want me to know.'

'They're all like that,' Laila said.

'Who are?'

'Grown–ups. They're like kids. They think they can keep a secret when everyone knows about it.'

'But I want to know what it is!'

'That's what I mean,' Laila said. 'You want to be like the grown–ups.'

'How?'

'You wanna be a kid.'

We were giggling away in our own worlds when I noticed Donna and Chloe up the road, coming towards us. There were a couple of boys and another girl with them who I didn't recognise. I elbowed Laila and said, 'We've got trouble.'

'It's your gang again,' she replied.

'Yeh, my gang,' I sighed.

Donna and her crew stopped before they got to us. They started discussing something among themselves and then approached us menacingly.

I felt a strange tingling on my neck - as if I was being watched. I looked back at the mosque. Someone was looking at us. I blinked and there was no one there.

The mosque's doors opened and a load of men came out.

Shamshad

When I saw Karen and Laila on the other side of the road from the mosque, I hated Karen more than anything in the world. She had stolen my best friend. I prayed that Karen would be given a hiding by her old gang. I recognised Donna even from where I was. But it was not to be. Too many people came out of the mosque at the same time.

I went back into the class and started snapping at the kids as they tried to recite the Holy Quran. Part of me wanted to go out, right there and then, and give Karen a piece of my mind, and part of me wanted to let Laila know what I thought of *her* now.

The day dragged on and on, and no matter how hard I tried to forget about what had happened, I just couldn't do it.

On the way home, I sat in the back seat of the car thinking about what Dad had done to her with the cane. Why didn't he just hit her with it? Why did he lift her face up, as if there was anything in it to see?

Looking at me through the rear mirror, Dad said, 'You know you are not allowed to have anything to do with any member of Lucky's family.'

How many times had I been told this. The reasons were all jumbled up inside my head. We were *Jats*, landowners, with lots of land in Pakistan. Three of my cousins are in jail over there. Someone in Lucky's family had dishonoured someone in ours. Somebody died in Pakistan. We hated them. They hated us. And none of them could be trusted. But there was something else, something unspoken about us and them. Everyone knew that my Dad and her Dad had once been friends, but this was never talked about, in what little was talked about in my house. Even the mention of their family name sent the silence of my house into a deeper well. I wanted to know what this secret thing was, but I knew I was meant to keep well away from Karen.

'I hate her, Dad, I hate her!' I snapped. 'I don't know why she came.'

Dad released me from his stare and I looked out at a woman pushing a baby in a pram. The baby was crying. The woman gently lifted it out, kissed it and hugged it. I wanted to be in a pram with Mum pushing me.

Dad parked the car outside our house, leaned over and looked at me. I was expecting him to tell me off, like he'd read my thoughts, but he had a warm look in his usually cold, black eyes. His thick, raised brows showed the grey roots of the blackened hairs.

'I've been meaning to buy you this,' Dad said leaning back to the space in front of the front passenger's seat.

'You've finally got me a new laptop, Dad,' I thought, 'you're so transparent.'

'I know you might not believe me, but I am so proud of the fact that you came top in the school chess tournament,' Dad said, putting his hand into the bag.

'That was last year, Dad,' I thought with a sinking heart.

'We invented *shatrange*, chess, and not the *goray*.' Dad paused to look at me for a reaction.

I gave him the best false smile I could muster, thinking, 'Yes Dad, you've told me this a thousand times.'

Dad continued, 'Chess is such a great way to learn about strategy and planning. And I still remember how you taught me that the quickest check, what do you call it, is foolish mate…'

'Fool's, mate, Dad.'

'Yeh, fool's, mate, that's in four moves.'

'Two, Dad.'

'Yes, the old mates of mine are getting into a bit of chess and I want to show them how it can be done in four.'

'It's in two, not four, Dad.'

'No, that's impossible.'

'Come on, hurry up,' I thought. 'I think I know what's in that bag.'

Handing me a chess set, Dad said, 'These pieces were hand-carved in Pakistan.'

'That's really great, Dad,' I said, taking the chess set from him. 'Just what I wanted.'

'Really! I knew, I just knew,' Dad said. 'Will you show me the moves?'

'White pawn to F3. Black pawn to E6. White pawn to G4. Black Queen to H4. Check mate!' I said quickly. Dad smiled, a stupid *Ireallydontunderstand* type of a smile.

'The great thing about playing chess is that you have to plan out what you want to do. Life is like that. It requires hard skills. We have to set our goals and follow them. Do you understand, Shamshad?'

'Yes Dad, I understand.'

'Love is a soft thing, and to survive in this world we need hard things, strength, thinking tactics. Love is beautiful, but it is not enough. Though I do love you, Shamshad, I want you to be strong.'

'I understand, Dad. And did you just say you love me?'

Dad smiled. 'I did.' He looked as astonished as me.

Just then, Dad's mobile rang. I went inside. As I opened the door, I saw Mum walking out of the living room, heading for the kitchen. Skype, I thought. If it was just me and she noticed I had come in, she would have shut the door and carried on. But when Dad came back, she always turned the computer off and entered into the kitchen.

Dad walked in. He was still talking on the mobile, his face beaming.

Giving me a twenty-pound note, he said quickly, 'Second sale in two days. Things are picking up for Medina Estates.'

I took the money and stepped aside as he walked into the living room. My Dad's company, Medina Estates, was the oldest estate agency in Boarhead East. It wasn't just an estate agency. We did money transfers to Pakistan and sold airline tickets, rented property and sold insurance.

He was in such a good mood today, I saw my chance. Mum was bringing in his tea. I took the tea from Mum and gave it to Dad. He was still on the mobile. Putting the tea on the coffee table in front of him, I prayed inside my head, 'Please God make it another sale.'

I sat down in front of him, fidgeting with the twenty-pound note. When he finished, I asked, 'Another sale, Dad?'

'No, silly,' he said. 'Baba Zaman just had a new baby.'

Everyone knew Baba Zaman. He was the first one to move to Boarhead from Pakistan. He walked with a bent back. He coughed all the time, spitting phlegm on the ground. He was on wife number three or four; the others were all buried in the graveyard.

'How's the baby?' I asked.

'Alright, I think,' Dad said sadly, sipping his tea. 'It's a girl.' He quickly added, 'Such is Allah's will.'

'And the new Mum?' I asked.

'She's young, she'll be alright,' Dad said. 'You're asking a lot of questions today.'

I don't know where I got the courage from, but I said, 'I'm fourteen now Dad, not young any more...'

'An old woman, eh,' he interrupted with a laugh.

'It's not important, Dad, but it's been bothering me, like. Were you and Karen's Dad once best mates? I asked Mum and she said to ask you.'

Dad called Mum, 'Sakina, in here now!' I stood up and stepped toward the door.

Mum came running in. Dad took his shoe off and held it in his hand, shouting, 'What have I said about talking about that family?'

'She's growing up. She keeps asking questions. I always tell her to ask her father, as you know best,' Mum said.

'How dare you disobey me!'

Dad stepped towards Mum. He raised the hand with the shoe. She lowered her head.

'It's my fault, Dad, honest. I couldn't help it. I'll never ask again,' I said. He looked at me with raging eyes.

I ran upstairs, plugged my headphones in and listened to Lady Gaga.

Kiran

Even though Shamshad was always horrible to me, I still felt sorry for her. When I told this to Laila, she said, 'Maybe she was found in a dustbin?'

'Maybe,' I said, thinking about how my Mum could just flip from one mood to another.

'Mums,' Laila laughed, 'can't live with 'em.'

'Can't live without 'em,' I added.

Laila and I chatted all the way to Boarhead College. I told her what Donna had done to me, Laila shook her head in disbelief. It was like we'd been best friends all our lives.

I had never been to the college but Laila knew her way round. We went down a flight of stairs, along a corridor into the women's toilets and Laila taught me how to do my *voozu*, to clean myself up before prayers. After that, we went into a large room. There were kids from East Boarhead, people from Africa and even some white people. Most of the women wore hijabs. The men had beards. Some of them wore long skirts; some wore *shalwars* that ended above their ankles.

Someone tapped on a microphone, and a white man, in his early twenties, stood up on the platform. He had light-brown, unkempt hair and a small, stubbly beard. His thin face reminded me of the pictures of Jesus. Everyone went silent. He gave the call to prayer, the *azaan*. I had heard this at my grandfather's and often on the television, but never as beautiful as this. It was like he was singing something that was coming from deep inside me. After the *azaan* in Arabic, he did it in English.

By the time the *azaan* finished, the men had placed mats on the floor. Some people sat at the back but most stood in neat lines on the mats. Women on one side, men on the other. I stood next to Laila and we all prayed.

After the prayers, we all squatted down and the white man who had given the *azaan* began to speak: 'Brothers and sisters, may peace be upon you all. How many of you heard the *azaan* in English for the first time?'

Along with a few others, I put my hand up. He looked around, stroked his beard, and said, '*Allah O Akbar*, Allah is great. It means no one is greater than Allah. This means we are all equal in the eyes of Allah. When we prostrate, we do so as equals. In this equality, we seek peace for us and justice for mankind. And why do we get together five times a day to pray? This is so that five times a day we have a chance to get organised and find peace.'

He paused and pointed at the posters around the room. The words Kashmir, Chechnya, Iraq, Afghanistan, Somalia, Lebanon and Palestine were written in large letters. Underneath them were pictures of destruction and horrible injuries.

He continued, 'And we pray for an end to suffering. For those of you who have come here for the first time, I would like you to note there is no picture of God, nor of our Holy Prophet, may peace be upon him, nor of Jesus, may peace be upon him.'

He paused again, and said with a sly laugh, 'And he was an Arab. Not a blond-haired, blue-eyed boy from up the road. And don't any of you dare to think I look like him!'

Someone laughed but I froze, thinking he was talking about me.

He continued, 'And Jesus, may peace be upon him, felt it is duty to stand up against Rome…'

A man's voice from the audience interrupted, 'Didn't Jesus say, "Render unto Caesar that which is Caesar's"?'

The speaker brushed a lock of hair off his forehead, smiled at the questioner and nodding said, 'It's true, brother. But Jesus also said, "And unto God, that which is God's. And what is God's? Life is God's. Everything is His." But what did Rome think? That he was a threat. Yes it did. And did he not stand up for God? Yes he did. Did he not stand up against the West? Yes he did. Today, the West is sending its crusading armies to invade Muslim lands. Is it not our duty to follow in the tradition of our prophets?'

Everyone clapped. Waving a leaflet in his hand, he said, 'The crusader, this country's Prime Minister, is coming to Manchester next week. We call upon all believers to go and protest against him.'

As we left, Laila took some leaflets and said we could give them out at school. On the way home, I asked her, 'I'm not sure about all this crusader stuff.'

'They get a bit hot-headed, this lot, and don't make sense,' she replied, 'and sometimes they're the only ones who do make sense.'

When I got home, I said a loud *himumhidadI'mhome* and without waiting for a reply, I ran upstairs and slumped onto my bed and started listening to Lady Gaga.

I heard the front door slamming shut and smiled, that had to be Dad. By the time I got downstairs, he was already watching the television, beer can in hand.

'Dad, can I go to Manchester for the day on Saturday?'

'Where were you all day today?' Dad asked.

'I went to a meeting and learned how to pray properly, and learned what the *azaan* means.'

He went into a deep silence.

'Can I go or not?' I asked.

He rubbed his hand across his face and nodded. I turned around to leave, and he said, 'Do you want another fiver?'

'I still haven't spent the one you gave me.'

'You've become so honest with all this hijab stuff,' he laughed. I picked up a cushion and chucked it at him.

On the way to dropping me off at Boarhead station, Dad said, 'Just be careful in Manchester.'

'I will, Dad,' I said. 'I will.'

As the train set off, I thought how Boarhead was a world of its own. To get here by car, you come via a motorway, which runs along the side of a hill. Boarhead is hidden behind the hill. If you come by train, the rail track is on the other side of another hill, an even bigger one than the motorway one.

I arrived early and went for a wander down Market Street. I got a text from Laila: *Running 15 mins late.* I was about to reply when I saw them. Jake and his mates were coming towards me. Shamshad was with him, her arm in his. She was wearing a low-cut top and a short flowery skirt, and had a black bag on her shoulder. She kept shaking her head to push her hair off her face. They stopped by an ice-cream van and ordered. Shamshad giggled each time Jake said anything. She had bright lipstick and thick eyeliner on. I was about to turn around and leave when she saw me looking at her.

Jake whispered something in her ear. She smiled without taking her eyes off me, and then Jake yanked her arm and they went in the opposite direction. Shamshad kept turning around to look at me as they disappeared into the crowd of shoppers.

Shamshad

When Karen saw me with Jake, I could have just died. I kept looking over my shoulder, convinced that Karen would follow me. Jake kept asking me what the matter was, but I kept quiet. After a while, Jake got fed up with me and went off with his mates. I changed back into my normal clothes at Piccadilly station and went back home. Before catching the train, I threw my skirt and top into a bin.

Dad was out. Mum was on Skype. She shut the door to the living room when I came in. I went into the bathroom and cleaned my teeth over and over again, trying to chase the taste of vodka away. I scrubbed my teeth until my gums bled, trying to remove the stench of cigarettes, all the while begging the Almighty to forgive me. 'I have been bad, Almighty,' I prayed. 'You are merciful. All-forgiving. Forgive me. Forgive me.'

I did my *wudhu*, cleaned myself, and readied myself to pray. I went to my bedroom, spread my prayer mat on the floor and prayed. Rani came into the room as I prayed and curled up next to me. After I had finished, I picked her up and stroked her from her head all the way to her tail. She closed her eyes and pushed her head up against mine, arching her back as my hand went over it.

As I stroked Rani, I heard Mum laughing downstairs. It's a sound I rarely hear and it made me think about the one time she really, really made me happy. It was on a Friday when I saw a side of Mum I would never have dreamt existed. I'd just come home from school and was expecting her to be, as ever, glued to the computer screen, yapping away to some goat-herder in Pakistan on Skype, but she was standing by the window, looking out on the street and waved at me as soon as she saw me.

She opened the front door and said, taking my school bag from me, 'Come on, Shamshad, we're going.'

There was a decisiveness in her voice I had not heard before. For a moment, I thought maybe she'd had a big fight with Dad and was leaving the house, but then I looked in her eyes. They looked like the eyes of a woman much younger than my Mum. Mischievous eyes. Determined eyes. But one about to leave home? No.

Mum quickly hung my school bag onto a hook, picked up a large brown bag that was behind the door, and said in English, something she rarely did, 'Swimming.'

'Swimming!' I almost jumped out of my skin. My Mum and swimming! She grabbed my hand, giggled and slammed the door shut behind us.

Before I could get myself together, a white van, full of *buddies* – old women – from our neighbourhood pulled up outside our house and Mum shoved me inside and then got in herself. The amount of noise these buddies made on the way to the baths would put an army of hormonal teenagers to shame. And the words they used, about each other and about the men they saw on the way? May the Almighty forgive them, especially my Mum.

The baths were even noisier than the van. They were heaving with happy women and kids. I have never seen so many bums, bigger than coffee tables, tree trunk legs wobblier than jelly jumping into water, ignoring the whistles of the irate lifeguards.

Mum handed me a plastic bag with my towel and a new swimsuit in it, kissed me on the forehead and rushed off to change, along the way waving to a big, fat woman who was standing on the edge of the pool, slightly bent, with one foot touching the top of the water. The woman was wearing a purple swimsuit, leggings and a matching top that came down from a tight hood from her head to her waist.

This was the first time I had been here since the Victoria Baths had been modernised. The old swimming pool in the middle with changing cubicles all around was still here, but now two larger pools, one with diving boards as well as slides and water features for children, had been built. The old ceiling, with its long beams, had been replaced by a much taller glass one.

Mum had bought me a normal, dark blue swimming suit with a matching cap. I got changed as quickly as I could and when I came out, Mum was waiting for me outside my cubicle. I put my hand to my mouth as soon as I saw her. I was expecting her to be dressed like her purple-suited friend, but Mum was wearing a swimsuit like mine, with one of Dad's large white t-shirts on top. She burst out laughing when she saw me looking at her.

Mum was like an excited girl and I felt like the adult. She hopped over to the deep pool and as she was about to jump in, a lifeguard dressed in a bright yellow top and red shorts whistled at us. The guard pointed at Mum and waved her index finger telling us not to do what Mum was about to do. I was a bit puzzled and tried to work out what it was we had done, when Mum took off the t-shirt, and said, nodding to the lifeguard, 'This one, she doesn't let us go into the water with normal t-shirts on.'

'You've been here before, Mum?!' I asked incredulously.

'But not with you,' she said rolling up the t-shirt and lobbing it towards a bench on the side, behind the lifeguard.

As she jumped into the water I shouted, 'It's the deep end, Mum.'

She went down into the water and then when her head popped out she said, 'Race you to the other end.'

'You've no chance,' I said, jumping in next to her.

I was wrong. Mum swam like a fish, doing her doggy paddle, panting and splashing all the way to the other end of the pool. She beat me, but she was really out of breath.

We did a couple of slow lengths, me showing off my breaststroke, front and back crawls and butterfly. Mum stuck to her doggy paddle.

When we stopped for a breather, Mum pointed at the tall diving board in the pool behind us and said, 'Let's jump from that one.'

'It's much higher than it looks from here, Mum.' But she had already got out of the water.

As we walked towards the queue for the jump, a lifeguard stopped us. 'Why won't she let me go?' Mum asked me.

I asked the lifeguard what the matter was and she replied, 'Everyone has to swim a width before they are allowed to jump.'

I translated for Mum and she lowered herself gently into the water and swam across to the other end. I followed her.

Waiting in the queue, I began to feel goose pimples. I hate heights, but didn't want to let Mum down.

'It's all right if you don't want to jump,' Mum said, walking up the steps. 'I might not be able to do it when I get to the top, so you wait here and get ready to pull me out of the water if I do manage to do it.'

'OK, Mum.'

'And don't laugh at me if I can't.'

'OK, Mum,' I laughed.

Mum looked at a woman who was waiting at the edge of the high jump. She was a skinny, blonde-haired woman who kept looking down, then moving away towards the steps only to go back again. She did this a few times and then came down the stairs, crying.

When Mum's turn came, she went up the stairs, walked onto the platform and jumped straight off, without waiting or thinking. She came down making a lot of noise. It was difficult to tell whether she was screaming in fear or joy. She landed in the water with a great big splash. I was relieved when her head emerged out of the water. She swam towards some steps close to me.

Climbing out of the water, she said, 'I did it.'

She looked round the pools and said, 'Do you want a go?' I shook my head.

'Then I don't either,' Mum said.

I was so deep in thought, remembering my one special time with Mum that I didn't hear her calling me at first.

'Yes, Mum,' I replied loudly.

'You left the bathroom sink dirty,' she said. 'Sorry, Mum.'

I felt all unclean again; I held my hands open in prayer, and prayed, 'Almighty, forgive me for what I have done. I will never do it again.'

Karen's face flashed through my mind, and I slammed my hand on the side of the table. Rani jumped out of my lap.

Kiran

'What's Shamshad like?' I kept thinking, waiting for Lalla. As soon as I saw her, I told her about Shamshad and Jake. She said, 'Nothing surprises me about her.'

Though neither of us admitted it to the other, we didn't want to bump into Shamshad. We messed around for a little while then went home.

The next morning I put on a clean headscarf and left for school. Shamshad was waiting at the top of our street, on the other side of the road. At first, I didn't believe my eyes and looked at her again. She stood on the other side of the road, unconcerned by all the eyes staring at her. Her arms were folded across her chest.

I quickened my pace. She did the same. I started running. She did the same. I ran as fast as I could and stopped by Mrs Johnston, the lollipop lady, at the top of our road. Shamshad was beside me. Panting. I moved closer to a woman with two children and crossed the road. I could feel Shamshad's breath on the back of my neck. I went along the main road instead of the short cut to the bus stop. Shamshad followed me all the way.

At the bus stop there were lots of kids, many of them going to our school. I bought my weekly bus pass from the driver and went to sit down, feeling relieved as most of the seats had someone sitting on them. I sat next to an old lady. As I was sitting down, she handed me a bag and said, 'Can you help me off with this, love.' I took her bag and moved back whilst she got up off the seat.

Shamshad sat down next to me, stuck her elbow into my ribs and hissed, 'Keep that little trap of yours shut!' I kept quiet.

'Is she wearing her mini-skirt again?' Aisha glared her braced teeth at me.

Digging her elbow into me even harder, Shamshad said, 'She's better now. I'm teaching her to be proper.'

I squealed. The cronies laughed. Aisha laughed the loudest. Shamshad stepped on my foot as hard as she could before getting up to leave.

I went to the toilets and washed my face before going to class. Everyone was staring at me when I entered. But for a slight clicking noise, it was really quiet, like everyone was holding their breath for a big bang. I wanted to yell, 'What have I ever done to any of you?' but I couldn't say anything.

My feet felt really heavy, my side ached and I felt the weight of all those eyes glaring at me. Tears began to burn in my eyes. 'Don't cry in front of this lot, Kiran,' I said to myself. 'Don't you cry, girl. They're just ignorant. They're just making you the fool.'

When I got to the desk, I saw what the joke was. Everyone started laughing. A small toy monkey, wearing a hijab over a mini-skirt, was dancing on my desk.

'Very funny,' I said as I picked it up. I gave Aisha a dirty look. She stopped laughing. I turned off the monkey and opened my bag - then realised that my pencil case was still in my locker. I looked at the clock. There were still five minutes to go and I rushed out. Someone clapped, then everyone clapped. When I got to the door, Shamshad was standing there, peeping in. She grabbed me by the collar, pulled me away from the door and slapped me hard across my face, snarling, 'How dare you spread lies about me.'

'I haven't told anyone, I swear,' I said.

She was about to hit me again, when I heard Mr Mayflower's shoes clicking on the tiles. He walked with a limp. The sound was unmistakably his. Shamshad let go of me.

'Shouldn't you girls be in class?' Mr Mayflower said.

'I just came to borrow something, sir,' Shamshad said.

'Very good. Very good,' Mr Mayflower replied in his usual manner. 'You look a bit sore this morning, Karen,' he said to me.

'I left my pencil case in my locker, Mr Mayflower,' I said.

'Very good. Very good. Chop chop, now. Go and get it,' he told me. 'And you can carry on chatting at break.'

'Yes, *Karen*, I'll see you at break,' Shamshad said, running towards her class, the echo of her feet fading down the corridor.

I didn't pay any attention to Mr Mayflower's lesson. He didn't notice these things. He just looked out from his thick glasses, brushed his wild hair off his head when it fell forward and carried on with whatever he was going to do. I tried not to think about the coming break by thinking instead about the stories that went around about Mr Mayflower. You could make any excuse to him and he would believe you. He was a legend in our school for being the dopiest of teachers. However, Mr Mayflower couldn't stop break from coming round. I had only told Laila, and she had promised not to repeat it.

'I didn't say a word to anyone,' Laila said when I saw her at break. She was carrying a plastic bag in her hand. Then she smirked, 'Except for mentioning it on my Facebook wall...'

'How could you, Laila?' I protested, looking round for Shamshad.

'Don't worry about her for a bit,' Laila said. 'She and Jake have gone to Mrs Seaver'. Mrs Seaver is the Head. I was about to ask why when Laila grabbed my hand, led me towards a covered area, and said, 'That's why.'

Someone had written: *Shamshad fancies Jake.* 'Ouch,' I said.

Laila laughed, 'Sorry, cross my heart and hope to die.'

'Cow!' I swore.

'Moo,' Laila grinned, then she added, 'Come on, are you going to help me give the leaflets out?'

'Just you and me?' I asked.

'There's a few others,' Laila said.

'Are we allowed?'

'No one will know who did it,' Laila said. 'We'll do it quickly.'

'Well, nothing much's going right for me,' I said. 'Besides, you're really good at keeping secrets.'

Putting some leaflets into my hand, Laila said, 'Moo.'

Past the covered area, our school grounds are dotted with trees, which go all the way down towards a farm, where cows often sit, staring at us, chewing their cud. Kids from West Boarhead hang out under the birches, and the East Boarhead lot hang out at the opposite end, by the poplars.

We had hardly given any leaflets out when Donna, Chloe and Megan came towards us. Jake was a few steps behind them, coming from the direction of the covered area. He was talking to Shamshad. Behind Jake, kids from West Boarhead were standing around close to each other. Fluff from the birch tree was blowing in the wind like snowballs.

I was handing leaflets to some Muslim boys from Year 8 when Donna came up to me, grabbed the leaflets out of my hand and swore. I tried to snatch the leaflets back; she pushed me in the chest. I steadied myself. Donna's chubby cheeks were red. Wiping her blonde hair off her face, she stared at me with raging eyes and said, 'Showing your colours, eh.'

'Get lost, Donna,' I said, putting my arm around Laila. 'Just go away.' The crucifix drawn on my forehead began to sting.

Girls and boys from West Boarhead ran down towards us.

Chloe pointed at us with her index finger and then rubbed it across her neck as if it was a knife, hissing, 'Talibans.'

Donna crumpled the leaflets she had taken from me, threw them to the ground and turned towards Laila saying, 'You should be supporting our lads in Afghan.'

Laila's face reddened. She said, 'British soldiers went to my granddad's house in our village in Kandahar. Shot him in front of everyone. One of them put his boot on my granddad's head and had his photo taken. Did he come to Boarhead and bomb it?'

'If you don't like it here, why don't you…'

Muslim boys and girls from East Boarhead had come round as well. Laila and I were between two heaving lines.

'Terrorists,' someone shouted from the East Boarhead line.

'Up yours, Osama.' Megan pointed to a turbaned Sikh from Year 8.

Donna turned around and shouted over to Jake, who was still talking to Shamshad, 'Jake, come here, right now.' Jake ran over. Shamshad went back into school.

Above us, the wind stopped. The air filled with a seething anger. Some boys pushed each other, swearing. I looked at the West Boarhead line. It was thicker than ours, and getting bigger. Jake came and stood next to Donna. She pointed her fat finger at our line, and shouted, 'If you lot don't like it here, go back to Shariaistatan or wherever you come from.' The angry silence from above came down and engulfed us. Donna's eyes filled with tears and she said in broken words, 'My Dex is out there in Afghanistan, getting shot at by youse lot. And some of you know Dex, don't you?' She held Jake's hand, jabbed her finger at me and said, 'And you know him well, don't you? I don't know if he's alive or dead now, do I?'

There was a gasp from the western line. Jake said, 'Our Dex is missing. They think he might be dead or captured and taken to Pakistan…'

Donna's eyes narrowed. She stared at us and threatened: 'And if something happens to Dex, I'll have one of you.'

Jake shook his head. 'I didn't want our kid to join and I didn't want him to go.'

'What've you become?' Donna stepped away from Jake, looked him in the face and shouted, 'He's your brother and was just doing his job…'

'Doing what?' Jake interrupted.

Donna gritted her teeth.

Megan put her arm in Donna's, spat at Jake and, 'You Paki-loving traitor.'

'Donna, I love our Dex and you know that and I know you love him…'

'He should be with you here, Donna,' Laila said.

'He should,' Donna cried. 'But he might be dead.'

'He's alive, I know he is,' Jake said.

The Head came charging up towards us with an army of teachers behind her. Everyone ran off in all directions.

I followed Laila and we went down past the poplars, and hid behind a bush. A large brown and white cow was sitting a few feet away from us on the other side of our grounds, staring at us with its big eyes.

After getting my breath back, I said to Laila, 'I'm sorry about your granddad. I didn't know.'

'How would you?' she said, pulling out a blade of grass. Putting it in her mouth, she whispered, 'It was my *dada*, me granddad. My Dad couldn't even get to his funeral.'

I pressed on her hand, and asked, 'When?"

'Exactly thirteen months and four days ago,' she said, spitting on the ground.

We sat in silence for a while. Laila had picked up a twig and was digging into the ground with it. I looked into the vacant eyes of the cow. A small bird had perched itself on the cow's head. The cow carried on chewing. A fly buzzed above it. It flicked its tail. The fly continued to buzz. The cow shook its head and the bird flew off.

Even though I was feeling calm on the outside, inside I was really, really mad. I was mad at Shamshad for tormenting me. I was mad at myself for not standing up for myself. Laila had just stood up to that nutcase. Why couldn't I? I was really angry with Mum for taking me to church. And my Dad, I thought, 'How could you be you?' And I was angry for Laila.

Just when I was thinking of her, she said, 'He was going to give water to a dying soldier, someone who had come from so far away and who had caused so much suffering to his village. He was going to give one of them water, and they killed him and took photographs.'

I didn't say anything. I searched for the right words, but all I could find was rage.

'That's what my Dad said happened,' Laila said. 'He doesn't say much any more, my Dad. He wants to go home, but there's no one there now. They brought bulldozers and flattened the village, they did. And everyone just went somewhere else. Some of us now live in Pakistan. That's what my Dad said they did.'

We walked silently back to our classroom. I took the bag with the leaflets from Laila and hid it under my jacket. After shoving the plastic bag into my locker, I went to my classroom and floated through English.

The whole school was called in for a special assembly that afternoon. Our assembly hall was a long, tall building. All along the wall were engraved names of past Heads and Head Boys and Girls. When empty, it echoed each time you took a step. Your voice, even in whispers, bounced around the room. The Head, a police officer and Mr Mayflower were sitting on the stage. Everyone filed in and sat down, class by class, looking stiffly towards the front. Nobody spoke as they entered. The teachers sat on the sides. Year 9s and 10s stood behind the teachers at the ends of the rows of chairs.

Mrs Seaver stood up and tapped on the microphone, three times. The noise from her fingers subdued the echoes. 'I think you know why you are here. I have a few words to say to you. As always in my assemblies, if you have a question to ask, you may do so. If you have something important to say, which we should all hear, you may say it. But first, we have a special guest here.' She nodded towards the police officer and continued, 'Chief Constable Sharon Brittle has come here, and has a few words to say to you. '

Mrs Seaver moved back from the microphone stand and gave it to the Chief Constable, who placed a folder in front of herself and said, 'I won't take up too much of your time, school. I know you have a lot of learning to do and are eager to get back to your classes.' She paused. A giggle rippled through the assembly. She smiled at us. 'Yes, that's how I felt when I was sitting where you are now.' The ripple rose a bit louder. Even Mrs Seaver smiled.

The Chief Constable continued, 'I am not here to teach you. Nor to preach to you. I am here to tell you simply about the law. All this week, I have been going to schools across the northwest, giving the same message. In this country, we have laws; it is my job to enforce them. In many schools, troublemakers from outside, with obvious support from inside, have been giving leaflets out about the Prime Minister's visit to Manchester. I know emotions are running very high about the war, especially around West and East Boarhead, from where many soldiers have gone to fight. They are doing their jobs. Whether they like it or not. I am doing mine. Whether I like or not. You are doing yours.' She paused, and said with another smile, 'And I know you like it.' Everyone laughed.

When the laughter subsided, she said, holding one of the leaflets we were handing out in the playground, 'We are lucky to live in a country that enjoys freedom of speech. Some of you have seen these. Some of you have been giving them out in this school. My job is to tell you that any child not at school during the forthcoming protests about the PM, and without a valid note from their school or their parents, will be treated as a lawbreaker, and will be dealt with accordingly.'

Someone clapped. I looked around. All the teachers were clapping. As were most students from East Boarhead.

I raised my hands involuntarily, but stopped before I clapped. I looked over at Shamshad. She was sitting with her fists clenched.

'Let me read you a sentence from this leaflet,' the Chief Constable said, consulting it. '"Stop the Crusade of the Western Armies".' She cleared her throat, looked across at us, and said, 'You are young and cannot understand the subliminal message embedded in this sentence. It is the soft edge of terrorism. It is the breeding ground of extremism, and we don't want any more 7/7s. This is where it hides. It is ideas like this from which it grows. At the back of the room, as Mrs Seaver said, I have left some literature that will help you to identify extremism. For those of you who want to make your point to the Prime Minister, let me assure you that when I meet him in Manchester, I will let him know the strength of feelings about the government's policies. And, finally, I want to warn you again. Anyone breaking the law will be held accountable.'

She turned to Mrs Seaver and thanked her, and then walked off the stage. Her footsteps sounded all round the hall as she walked down the centre and out of the back.

When the police officer had left, Mrs Seaver said, 'In all my years, I have never called an assembly like this.' She stopped and looked down at us. Her gaze cut through the fading echoes of her cold voice. Someone coughed. Mrs Seaver continued, 'We have children from 85 countries in this school. We have 15 languages. Yes, this is a Christian school. We pride ourselves on this. There are many of you who are Muslims in our school and we welcome you. We celebrate Eid. And there are Hindus and Sikhs. And we celebrate Diwali and Vaisakhi. We try our best to accommodate everyone's faith here. We do this because we *are* a Christian School. And Christ taught us to love. To love each other. To love peace. And even on the Cross, he forgave. That is what we have tried to teach all of you in this school.'

She waited a moment, then went on, in a slightly softer tone: 'Now, children, it is good to have different opinions, but we want to be able to discuss these in a healthy atmosphere. It makes all of us stronger. Especially in the spirit of Christ. It is not about West and East. I want us all to be one happy family. Now, as always, I believe when passions are high we should let them vent. Those of you who feel they have an important question to raise or something to say, why don't you say it right now?' She stopped.

The assembly sank into a deep silence. I looked across at Laila. She was crying. I don't know why I did it, but I stuck my hand up. Mrs Seaver reared her head back, as though startled. She thought for a moment, then said, 'Yes - Karen, isn't it?'

'It's Kiran, Mrs Seaver,' I said. A few people laughed. Shamshad coughed.

'Stand up,' Mrs Seaver ordered.

My legs turned to jelly. Sweat tricked down my spine. Holding on to the chair in front of me, I pushed myself up.

'The Romans were westerners, yeah, Mrs Seaver? And did Jesus not stand up to them?'

From the corner of my eye, I saw Laila clap. A few others from East Boarhead joined in. I saw Jake. He clapped, and then suddenly stopped.

I was trembling. Sweat poured down my face. My shirt was stuck to my back. Everyone was staring at me.

'Well, Jesus certainly taught us to love one another and to forgive,' Mrs Seaver said as I sat down. 'But Jesus would not allow for unauthorised absence from my school.'

The tension broke and everyone laughed. I joined in as well. Mrs Seaver always managed to find a way of saying things at the end of an assembly that were funny.

I hurried out of school that day. Everyone was staring at me in a strange sort of way. I really wanted to walk out with Laila, but her Dad was picking her up and I was scared of Shamshad. She had many reasons now for getting at me. I saw Jake coming out of the door. He waved at me to stop, but I pretended I hadn't seen him, lowered my head and carried on. Two white boys blocked my path just as I was leaving the school gates. One of them was taller than the other. The tall one had curly red hair and a stubbly face. The shorter one was stocky, with short, cropped hair. They were Year 9s or 10s. I didn't know their names.

As I stepped off the pavement to get past them, one of them, the short–haired boy, moved aside and said, 'You don't need to do that.'

I stopped.

The taller one said, 'I wish I was as brave as you.'

I was trying to digest the compliment when the shorter one scratched his head, and said, 'Tony Blair lied to us. Me Dad went to Iraq and never came back.'

'Year 10 are going on the demo,' the tall one said.

I stepped forward and hugged him.

The short one laughed and said, 'I didn't know you did that.'

'What do you mean?' I asked, pulling away.

'Scarfies and hugging… scarfies…'

'Oh, get lost,' I said, wiping away tears of relief.

As the two boys left, Jake put his hand on my shoulder. I turned around. Behind him, still in the school grounds, Shamshad was giving me the evil eye.

Shamshad

I couldn't take my eyes off Karen, with Jake's hand on her shoulder. I thought back to what had happened. The whole world knew. It was all over Facebook. When I saw Karen in Manchester, I kept looking back at her. I didn't know how long she had been spying on me, but I was sure she had taken photographs of me with Jake on her mobile. I was going to get them deleted before they went up as well.

I hid in the toilets at the start of the dinner break. I cried, and swore to really, really teach her a lesson. I was sitting in the cubicle when I heard some girls talking about a big fight coming up in the playground. I wouldn't have cared, but someone mentioned Laila. I waited until they had left and went into the playground through the back entrance of the main hall. Everyone was walking down towards the other end of the grounds. It looked like East Boarhead was already there and West Boarhead was coming from all over. I was behind West Boarhead.

I stopped and thought about turning around. Two long lines had formed. I was about to turn and leave when Jake came up behind me. I felt so ashamed when I saw him, and stared down at the patches of chewing gum splattered onto the paved ground.

'I need to ask you something,' he said.

There was a lot of shouting and swearing coming from the lines in front of us.

'I promise I didn't do anything, Jake!'

He looked at me, all confused. Maybe he didn't know about all the stuff on Facebook. His hair flew off his face. His earring glittered in the sunlight.

'You don't know, do you?' I said.

'Why did you write that stuff in the covered area?' Jake asked. I just died.

'It wasn't me!' I cried. 'It was her, that Karen. She saw us together in Manchester and she's jealous of us.' Jake's face turned red. He looked away from me. Someone was calling him.

Turning to me, he said, 'There is no *us*, Shamshad. You came out to let your hair down and mess about with me mates. That's all.'

'How could I have said what I just did?' I thought.

Jake held my hand and said, 'We're friends, aren't we?' I nodded.

'I need your help.'

'Anything,' I said.

He cleared his throat and said, 'It's about our Dex. I know your Dad's an important man. Can I come to your house and speak to him about our kid?'

'Oh no, please don't do that. Don't come to my house. You don't know my Dad. He'll kill me if he finds out about us.'

Jake held me by the shoulders, and said, 'Look, there's no *us*. I've told you. I want some help to find my brother.'

Someone called Jake again. He let go of me and went away. I remained standing where I was. Ashamed! I had made such a fool of myself.

*

When I saw her going home that day after the afternoon assembly, I could have killed her on the spot. Everyone was looking at her as if she was something really special. And now Jake was chasing after her as well. I promised myself, there and then, that I was going to kill Karen even if it meant spending the rest of my life in jail. I was going to kill her the next day. But I couldn't wait. When I saw her cooing up to Jake outside the school gates, I knew she could see me and was rubbing my nose in it. I got so angry. I took out a pair of scissors from my bag.

Kiran

'Sorry, Kiran,' Jake said, pressing my shoulder.

He was standing under a crab apple tree. I had gone past this tree so many times but only today noticed its bent, leafless branches dangling out over the pavement, shedding its walnut-sized, red apples onto the pavement.

I shrugged my shoulder, forcing him to take his hand off me. His hand slid down my arm and I felt the tips of his fingers on the tips of mine. I moved my hand away and stepped back from him, crushing some of the fallen crab apples under my feet. Jake put his hands in his pockets and kicked some of the fallen leaves. Shamshad was making her way towards us, fidgeting with something in her bag.

I looked Jake in the face. He seemed to have grown older. He turned his eyes away from me and glanced over at Shamshad. She knelt down and started tying her laces. A brown leaf twisted and turned in the air and landed on Jake's head, perching itself like a feather.

He took his hands out of his pockets, brushed the leaf off his head and told me, 'You're welcome back, you know. I mean we're still us. And I gave Donna a piece of my mind for what she did. I swear I did. I don't know why I didn't do anything. I just don't know. Sorry, Kiran.'

I suddenly got enraged with Jake. 'Oh yeah,' I thought to myself, 'I can just see it, Jake. Kiran the Muslim, one of the gang again, like nothing's happened, eh? I'm not who you think I am any more, Jake. Kiran was never WTM. And Karen is dead!'

'I know, Jake,' I said aloud. 'Thanks though.' Jake nodded.

'You really know how to say what you feel, girl,' I congratulated myself.

'I don't know what to do, Kiran,' Jake said. 'You know I'm not for all this war, but he's me brother.' His eyes filled with tears, and he said, 'Please help me.'

Shamshad was still tying her laces, her eyes still fixed on me. I wasn't going to look away from her. I'm tired of your games, Shamshad,' I wanted to shout. 'Really, really tired. Come and do whatever you want.'

Jake turned towards Shamshad, pointed at her, and said loudly, 'There's nothing going on between her and me.'

That was when Shamshad stood up and ran towards me, screaming.

I was trying to work out what to do when Jake grabbed her hand. She stumbled, and the scissors dropped onto the pavement. She fell, banging her head against a wall, her hand twisted behind her back. Her books spread out across the pavement, and her hijab had got caught in a privet bush above her.

Jake picked up the scissors, and said to Shamshad, 'What you doing with these?'

Shamshad pulled her knees up to her chest, placing her head on them; she hissed and then started to cry.

'Serves you right,' I thought. 'I ought to sock you one right in the gob.'

I untangled her hijab and gave it to her. She snatched it out of my hands and put it on her head. 'You could have hurt Kiran with these,' Jake said, waving the scissors in the air.

I held out my hand for her. She took it, and pulling herself up said, 'Thanks, *Karen.*'

I should have let go and let her fall, but I didn't. She stuffed her books into her bag and left.

There were piles of dried leaves huddled together here and there. A bird twittered in a tree close to me. I looked at a nest, but I couldn't see the bird. It was still singing somewhere close by. I smiled at the thought that I hadn't noticed the clouds clearing. The sun winked down through the leafless branches of the trees that lined the path of School Lane, which led from our school gates down to the main road.

The wind suddenly changed direction. It was a cold, biting wind. It pushed a pile of brown leaves towards us, along the pavement. They were twisting and turning as they came. More leaves fell off the trees all along the lane. Some small, hardly dead. Others large - larger than the size of my hand. A dog barked somewhere in the gardens, and I thought of Shamshad and shook my head. 'Oh God,' I prayed, 'free me from her. Is this too much to ask? This is the first and only thing I have really asked of you. Is it too much?'

'Come on, Kiran.' Jake brought me back down to earth.

He pulled me towards a huge pile of leaves that had collected around a discarded pram, then let go of me, and started kicking the leaves. He then bent down, picked up a pile of leaves, and tossed them into the air. I ran into the pile of leaves and I too started kicking them, shouting with joy. Jake stopped, and asked, 'What's the matter with you?'

'Me prayers just got answered,' I said.

'Barmy,' Jake said, joining me.

When we stopped kicking the leaves, I noticed Mrs *Getoffmystreet*. That's what we called her. She was always there by her gate each day before the start of school and at the end of the day, staring out at us with her arms folded across her chest like a wrestler, with a look that said, *getoffmystreet.* I looked her in the eyes, stuck my tongue out at her, and followed Jake as he ran down the lane. Shamshad was standing on her own at the bus stop, on the other side of the pelican crossing. I stopped.

'I'm going to tell her what I think of her,' Jake said, stepping into the road.

I pulled on his hand, and said, 'Lay off, Jake.'

He stepped back onto the pavement and looked me in the face. 'Just lay off,' I repeated.

I pressed the pelican-crossing button.

'What is it with you girls? Don't you know what's good for you?' A bus pulled up on the other side of the road.

'Girls are girls,' I said. 'Yeah,' he said. 'Yeah,' I said.

The bus pulled away. Shamshad was on it.

The pelican lights turned green, but we didn't cross the road. 'You coming to the willow tree later?' Jake asked.

'So the mob can make fun of me, eh?'

'There's no mob anymore.'

I pressed the pelican lights button again. Jake said, 'We've got a lot of things to sort out and there's…'

The lights changed and crossing the road, I said, 'No!'

Jake followed me, and said, 'Please. It's not what you think.'

Getting onto the pavement on the other side of the road, I quickened my pace. Another bus was coming. Jumping inside I said again, more loudly, 'No!'

There was hardly anyone on the bus. Jake sat on a seat in front of me. I touched the window with my forehead. The glass was cold. It started raining. At first just a few drops, which hit the windows and slid down past my face.

Moments later, the glass misted. I wiped it and saw Jake's reflection. He was looking at me, pleading with those blue eyes.

When his stop came, he stood up, looked at me, sat down again, and asked, 'Do you mind if I walk home with you?'

'Why?'

'Don't want to see Dad. He drinks even more since Dex went missing.'

Shamshad

'*Allahjee*, dear God, how can you let Karen humiliate me?' I thought. 'Why don't you throw a bolt of lightning at her and get rid of her right now?' I didn't try to hide myself from her. I just stood there. I knew Karen could tell I was watching her. I tried to cheer myself up with thoughts of cutting her throat with a knife, or putting my scissors into her stomach, pushing her under a bus, or running her over with a car. I laughed when I remembered I couldn't drive.

I was so angry I was trembling, especially when she jumped about kicking leaves with Jake. And what did the stupid little cow think she was doing, sticking her tongue out at that old lady?

I couldn't get Karen out of my mind all the way home on the bus. 'Killing you would be too easy, *Karen*,' I resolved. 'I have to find a way that would make you feel like I do. I don't know how you've done it so quickly, taking all my friends away from me, but I won't let you get away with it!'

I was so deep in thought that I missed my stop and ended up getting off at the top end of Boarhead East High Street. Our house was at the other end, past the restaurants and takeaways that lined both sides of the High Street. My Dad's office was in the centre of the High Street.

Mumtaz Ali Khan, the old man who lived in a house behind ours - Baba Khanu as everyone called him - nodded when he saw me walking past the window of Lala's Kebab House. I flashed a false smile back at him. He was a short, fat man, who had worked at Lala's before I was born. He waved at me with a hand covered in kebab mix and went back to spiking meat onto skewers and placing them into a refrigerated display. The door to Lala's was open. As I walked past it, I heard the meat sizzling on the grills. The scent of the roasting spicy meat made my mouth water. I slowed down.

A police helicopter came out of nowhere and started hovering above. A moment or so later I saw them. Men with masks on their faces, carrying English and Israeli flags, came charging down the middle of the High Street, shouting, 'Muslim Terrorists out of Boarhead!'

'Come inside, daughter, quickly,' Baba Khanu said, stepping out of the shop. Before I could say anything, he grabbed hold of me and yanked me inside the shop.

Four policemen on horses followed the masked men towards the town centre. After they were out of sight, Baba Khanu said, walking back behind the counter, 'Come, let me make you a big, fat kebab.'

'I'm not hungry, *Babaji*.'

'And if you're worried about your father, I'll phone him right now.'

Baba Khanu picked up a phone and spoke to my Dad. "He told me it's fine, as long as I don't charge you.'

Pushing a plate of kebabs and a can of Coke towards me, he said, 'It is so good to see you youngsters turning to Islam.'

'I didn't know I'd left it, *Babaji*,' I laughed, opening the Coke can. A bit of Coke sprayed onto the window. I took a sip. The fizz, the spice, the meat and the sugar: I was in heaven!

'I wasn't thinking of you,' Baba Khanu said, settling back again. 'I was thinking about Ghazanfer's granddaughter.'

Baba Ghazanfer's granddaughter, the name I had heard, but no face fitted it. A few drops of rain crashed against the window. I looked at the raindrops sliding down the glass and tried to work out who she was.

'You know, Liaqat Malik's Dad,' Baba Khanu said.

I couldn't work out who this was either. Suddenly it started pouring down.

'You know, he calls himself "Lucky". It's so good to see her leaving the church and coming back to our religion.' Baba Khanu said.

I put my hand to my mouth. I nearly choked. Karen's face flashed in front of my eyes.

'Oh God, why can't I get away from her?' I thought. I stared at Baba Khanu's reflection in the window. He moved slowly, his hands shaking a little. 'And yes, it's Kiran,' he told me. 'She won't let anyone call her Karen any more, like she used to.'

I was about to get up to leave, when Baba Khanu said, 'And Ghazanfer was here only yesterday. He has already been asked for her hand. From that handsome boy, Jani ...'

'What?' I stammered. 'Jani, my neighbour!'

'The Almighty works in strange ways indeed,' Baba Khanu said. 'Ghazanfer and Jani's father are going round to their house tonight.'

I settled back into my seat. I was hungry again. The food looked delicious and the beautiful rain was washing the world clean outside. I couldn't wait to finish my food. I wolfed it down. *Karen's marrying Jani* – I could see it written on the walls of the covered area at school. I was going to Photoshop her: in her bridal dress, head bowed, a photo of Jake in one hand and in the other, a photo of herself, in a headscarf, with a miniskirt, sitting next to her husband, Jani, dripping in his *sehra* of golden tinsels. And wasn't the bride-to-be going to love seeing Jake at her door!

After squeezing the last drops of Coke out of the can, I thanked Baba Khanu and walked, humming, out into the rain.

Kiran

The rain poured down the windows of the bus. Shamshad's face formed in the water. I heard the hiss of the doors opening, but was so engrossed in watching Shamshad's face being cut apart that I didn't realise it was my stop.

'What you planning to do, go all the way to Manchester?' Laila asked, boarding the bus. She looked at Jake, all puzzled, then looked at me and then back at Jake. I swear Jake blushed, but he turned his face away quickly and looked out of the window.

I grabbed my bag, saying to Jake, 'Aren't you coming, then?'

'No,' he said without turning around.

I didn't have time to work out what Jake was up to. Instead, I said sorry to the driver and got off the bus.

Laila came with me. She went into the bus shelter, stepping around a broken beer bottle, and said, 'Before you ask, you-know-who texted me.'

I laughed, following her into the shelter. An old lady, with curlers clearly visible under her flowery hat, gave us a *whatyoudoinghere* kind of a look and moved away from us, swinging her umbrella. I gave her a *whatyougonnadoaboutit* kind of a look back and then blocked her from my mind.

'It's not what you think,' I said to Laila.

'About what, Kiran?'

'About me and Jake, there's nothing, so stop thinking what you're thinking.'

'I *don't* think,' Laila giggled.

'Cow!' I said.

'Moo,' she replied, and we giggled. The old lady tutted, opened her umbrella and stepped out into the rain.

'What're you doing here, Laila?' I asked, getting out of the shelter and dodging the water dripping down from it.

'You were awesome in assembly. Awesome!' Laila said.

'You didn't come to tell me that.'

'Where did you get it all from?' Laila asked.

'I don't know,' I said. 'Maybe I've just had enough, or it's the meetings you've been taking me to.'

'Wicked,' Laila said.

'Lailoo, I got to get home. Mum'll be worried.'

'I told me Dad. He's going to pick me up from your house later,' Laila said. 'And you still got the miniskirt?'

I elbowed Laila in the ribs as hard as I could and ran. She raced after me, laughing and cursing. We stopped at the top of White Haven Road, which circled our estate. The road was lined with oak trees. Every now and again, overgrown branches of the trees would crack against the upper decks of buses and tall vans. On the opposite side of the road where I lived, ran the broken railings of East Boarhead Park.

Three boys were kicking a can to each other in the middle of St. George's Street.

The boys stared at us. Laila put her arm in mine. The boys started kicking the can to each other again. I knew them by face, but not by name. A dog barked somewhere close by. One of the boys said something that I didn't quite catch.

Laila squared up to him. He was a short, stocky boy, still in the uniform of St. George's Primary School. He had one foot on the can and both his hands were on his waist. He stepped back, he aimed and kicked the can at us. It missed us and hit a parked car.

A man swore from one of the houses and the boys ran off. The dog stopped barking.

Laila got a text. 'It's Jake,' she said.

'Texting you?'

'Cow!' Laila sniggered.

'Moo,' I laughed.

'Seriously, though,' Laila said, showing me Jake's text.

Kiran's mobile's off, Jake's text said.

I wrote back on Laila's mobile: *She's home.*

Liar, Jake texted back.

Where RU? I texted. *Across the road,* Jake wrote. And he was.

Laila waved at him to come over. He did, blushing, and asked suspiciously, 'Were you talking about me?'

'Nah,' Laila answered, and then dug her nails into my shoulders and whispered into my ear, 'Jake, eh?'

'I'm not proper like you,' I sniggered into her own ear. 'Remember.'

'*Khothee*,' Laila said, moving away from me.

I pulled her back and brayed loudly like a donkey.

'What's that mean?' Jake asked.

'Donkey,' I said.

'What does it mean, though?' he wanted to know.

Laila and I looked at each other. Jake answered himself: 'I'm a donkey, then, eh?'

Laila and I laughed.

'Will you help me find our Dex, Laila?'

'I don't even know what happens in my own house, so how can I help you find Dex in Afghanistan?'

'Someone must be able to help,' Jake said.

'Shamshad's Dad knows everyone in East Boarhead, you know,' I said. 'You should go to her house and ask her Dad.'

Leila stamped on my foot as Jake nodded and walked past us up the street.

It was only a short walk to our house, but we took ages to get there. When we got to the butcher's shop, I waved at Mr Mason, Elizabeth's husband. He's a tall, red-faced man with a big, bulging stomach. He was sharpening a knife and ignored me. Laila pulled a face at the half carcass of a pig dangling in the window. At first, I was puzzled, but then I remembered and did the same.

Pointing to my neighbour, I said, 'That's George. Sometimes he sits there like a stiff, other times he blasts out music for all the street to hear.'

Our house is in the middle of Willow Bank behind a row of manicured privet hedges, courtesy of George. He made sure the hedges were perfectly squared-off at the top, low enough for him to see out onto the street. No one at home minded, as it was one less job to nag Dad to do.

'Hi Elizabeth,' I shouted above the noise of George's music, closing the gate after Laila.

Mrs Elizabeth Mason was in her garden, hanging clothes out on the line. She looked across at us and then turned her back on us. Since I put the hijab on, she has stopped smiling at me, which was mostly what she did when we met.

I waved at George, who carried on staring at whatever he was staring at. His dog was sitting in its favourite position, its head on its front paws, its tired eyes focused on its master.

'Hi Bruno,' I called out to the dog.

The dog lifted its head a little towards me, moved its ear slightly and went back to its usual position.

‘Since I put on my headscarf,’ I said to Laila as we got inside my house, ‘so many of the neighbours have stopped talking to me.’

‘It’s a white thing,’ Laila said.

Mum had left me a note on the kitchen table: *Gone to pick some things up for tonight.*

Laila went straight for the fridge, took a can of Dad’s beer out, touched it to her face and laughed, ‘It happens to us he-ja-bees.’

‘You’re not going to have that, are you, Laila?’

She looked up at the clock, and said, ‘Don’t know. Got some time before Dad comes to pick me up.’

‘He’ll smell it on you, stupid.’

‘He won’t mind,’ Laila said, turning the beer can in her hand.

‘Won’t he!’ I said, incredulously.

‘Nah. Maybe just kill me,’ Laila grinned, putting the can back in the fridge.

We laughed about how, when we got on the buses, Asian women clocked us, and how we checked them back. We nattered about how some white men were scared of us little girls wearing a bit of cloth on our heads and how wonderful it would be to get away from Boarhead, especially during the coming Christmas holidays.

‘I’m going to meet my family in Pakistan this year,’ Laila told me. ‘No *Abbaji* Christmas for me.’

‘Lots of *Abbaji* Christmases for me,’ I said.

‘Why don’t you come as well?’ she asked.

‘Everyone’s here,’ I said. ‘My Dad never mentions going to Pakistan.’

‘Come with us,’ Laila repeated. ‘No Rudolf…’

‘I’ll ask,’ I promised.

We chatted about how Shamshad had been cut down to size. We roared and slapped our legs talking about how Jake thought he could get off with any girl.

Laila's father came too quickly. She had hardly got into the car when Jake texted me: *What u doing now?*

Me: *Who wants 2 know?* Jake: *Me* Me: *Who?* Jake: *Jake* 'He is so simple,' I thought.

I texted back: *Busy* Jake: *Old place* Me: *No* Jake: *Plz* Me: *No* Jake: *Plz. Plz* Me: *OK*

I went to see Jake. I reckoned all he wanted to do was to talk about Dex, and I had to get it into his thick skull that there was nothing I could do to help him. He was waiting for me at the top of our street.

'I thought you said by the tree,' I said.

Jake was lost deep in thought and we walked quietly up St. George's Street towards White Haven Road. Leaves were raining off the trees. There was hardly any traffic on the road. Just then, a red car came towards us. It slowed down as it approached. Someone who looked like Dex was sitting in the front passenger seat. He put his head out of the window and said something. I saw the driver's teeth.

As the car went past us, the Dex look-alike shouted at me, 'Go back home, you terrorist.'

A boy from the back of the car hurled a can of beer at me. It came flying through the air, leaving a trail of beer behind. It missed me and fell on the ground. Jake picked it up and ran after the car.

'Jake, stop!'

He kept running. When the car slowed down to let another car turn, Jake threw the can at the car. It hit its target and rolled under the wheels of an oncoming bus.

'It doesn't matter,' I said, when I got close to him.

'It does,' Jake said.

We crossed the road. 'Don't ask about Dex,' I said. 'I know nothing.'

'I know,' Jake said.

'If Dex was held by a Man U fan, then me Dad would probably know who he was,' I said.

'He might just be,' Jake grinned. 'Man U supporters are everywhere.'

We walked in silence to our favourite place. Jake pulled a twig out of the ground and said, twisting it in his fingers, 'I told him not to sign up for the army, but you know our kid, he's not one for listening. I didn't hear much from him after he went off to Afghanistan, not that I expected him to write anyway. But he never came back from a patrol, that's what I heard. I keep asking around, I know I must sound stupid, but I do and I don't know where Dex is still.

Yesterday, some men came to our house. Army men. Dad was his usual, drunk self. I had been waiting for the letter. They bring it round to the family, that's what happens. I've seen what it's like. Lots of them have been given out round here. I guess you know that, don't you? But they didn't give me a letter, Kiran. They said they knew I was going round asking for help to find our Dex, and told me to stay out of things I didn't understand.'

Throwing the twig as far as he could, Jake said, 'What should I do now, Kiran?'

I didn't know what to say.

He looked at me, and asked, 'What would you do if you were in my shoes?'

We stood under the willow tree for a while, and then Jake walked me back home. As I was leaving him, I said, 'Even though I hate Dex, I wish I could help you.'

'You know Taliban are Man U supporters...'

'Don't you dare come to my house again,' I said, slamming the door on Jake. I was mad at him. He was like a broken record. I ran upstairs, slumped on the bed and after a little while dozed off.

A heavy, booming voice woke me up. This was the unmistakable roar of my Granddad. It was dark outside. My room was all clean. My shoes were gone. The dirty towel had vanished. My dirty underwear was off the floor. My desk was all sorted, and everything that should be hanging on the hook behind the door was hanging there and not lying on the floor.

Each time Granddad met my Dad, it was like he hadn't seen him for years. Hugging and kissing, complaining to my Dad that so-and-so's-father's cousin died in Pakistan so he should go to their house in Sheffield to give them condolences; my father would always spend ages pretending to work out who this so-and-so was. A moment or so later, there was sure to be a heated argument between father and son.

Granddad saw me as I went past the front-room door. There was someone else in the room, but I didn't see who it was. Granddad raised his hand, but I shot into the kitchen before he could call me. The air in the kitchen was rich with the scent of fried samosas and pakoras. Below the noisy extractor, steam was coming out of three pans. Mum was putting some cups on a tray, next to a plate of freshly made kebabs.

'Wow, Mum,' I said, taking a samosa and biting into it. I asked, 'Why didn't you wake me up, and who's the special visitor?'

'You were out cold, you were, and don't talk with your mouth full,' Mum said. 'You're not a child now.' She picked up the tray with the tea, nodded to the plates, and said, 'Bring those in.'

The samosas were so delicious, I bit into another one. To Mum's disapproving eyes, I left the half eaten one on the table and followed her into the living room. Jani from Year 11 was sat down furiously texting on his phone. His father, who sat next to him, rocked his head continuously from side to side; I used to think this meant 'no' but it actually means 'yes'. My Granddad and Dad were arguing as they always did.

'If it wasn't for the Americans, where would your team be, lad?' Granddad asked, flicking his thick eyebrows at me, giving me that *hellosweetiejustkeepquiet* kind of a look.

Dad slapped the side of the chair and said, 'And look at your team, Dad. Where would your lot be if it wasn't for Arab money?'

Mum put the tray on the coffee table in between Granddad and Dad. I arranged the plates of food on the table, giving Jani a *whatthefyoudoinghere* stare. He looked away from me and sent his text. 'And how is my luv'ly granddaughter?' Granddad asked.

'And how grown-up you are now.'

Dad didn't give me a chance to reply and said, 'At least people across the world care for us. We're not merely have-beens, losers, acting-big-on-oil- money-from-Arab-fat-cats.'

'You know what I think about football?' I said, plonking the samosa plate on the table. 'How can anyone get excited about a load of big, sweaty men running around after a ball?'

Granddad laughed. Dad said, 'Man U is not just a football team, it's a legend…'

Granddad whispered into Mum's ear. Mum pulled away, took me by the hand and led me out of the room. As I was leaving, Jani's Dad said, 'Manchester United or Manchester City, we're all Muslims.'

In the kitchen, Mum said, 'Granddad wants you to dress properly for the occasion.'

'What occasion, Mum?'

Mum hesitated, then said, 'You know, dear, your Granddad has come with his friend and their son.'

'That loser, Jani, yeah,' I said. I didn't like where this was going.

'Well, you know.'

'Know what, Mum?'

Mum lifted the lid off a pan, waited for the steam to escape, stirred the food, and said, 'Your Granddad wants to know what you think about . . . about him arranging, you know, your marriage...'

'Mum!'

'Marriage?' I thought. 'They've got to be kidding. My parents have gone mad. I don't even know if they ever really got married themselves, or just pretended they were to keep everyone happy. An arranged marriage!'

'You know what Dad calls this sort of a thing?' I asked. 'A lucky bag job.'

'It's not my idea,' Mum said, putting the lid back on.

'Did you ever get married, Mum?'

'Oh, darling, how can you say such a horrible thing,' Mum grinned. 'Of course we did. I still have my dress.'

'You want me to wear it, do you?' She didn't answer.

'I'm only fourteen.'

'That's what I said,' Mum agreed, taking plates out of the cupboard. 'Your Granddad said it's just a thought for the future, not now.'

'To that idiot!' I snorted. And then I said: 'Why didn't you tell me before? At least I could have dressed *properly*?'

'Your Dad only told me last night...'

'Last night?' I hissed inside my head. I could throw the food away. No, spit in it. Chuck it at them. Then an idea came to me. 'How could *you* keep it from me, Mum?' I said, turning to leave.

'Where you going, luv?'

'To dress properly.' 'I'm sorry.'

'It's no big deal, Mum, honest.'

'Oh, Karey...'

'It's Kiran, Mum.'

I got changed as quickly as I could and came down to help Mum, wearing the shortest skirt I could find.

'That's my girl,' Mum said, her eyes almost popping out of her head.

Mum had cooked the chicken and was making fresh rotis. I chopped some salad and spread it out on a plate. Mum filled a large serving bowl with chicken, placed it on a tray with the rotis, put the plate of salad on top of the rotis and asked me to fetch a jug of water.

I took the empty plates, walked up to the front room and peeped in through the half-open door.

My Dad and Granddad were still arguing about Manchester United and City. Jani's Dad was smiling stupidly, stroking his hennaed beard. My Granddad stopped talking, closed his eyes and breathed in the aroma from the food. He opened his eyes, took off his glasses, took a handkerchief out of his top pocket and started cleaning them. Holding the glasses in his left hand, he pulled the table closer to him, and said, 'I could eat a horse and chase the jockey, I could.' Then he laughed loudly. He always said this when we put food in front of him in our house.

'I bet you could,' I thought, 'and probably take a bite out of the spectators as well.'

I walked in and said the loudest *As-salam alaykum* I had ever said. Jani's Dad's mouth dropped open when he saw me. My Dad looked at me and started wiping the table clean with a piece of tissue. Granddad put on his glasses, took them off and started polishing them again. Jani was still texting.

'Come on, girl,' I thought to myself. 'Fill a glass of water and chuck it at him. No, better to throw something hot so it'll burn.' When Mum brought in a steaming bowl of chicken, I imagined pouring it down his trousers. Jani screaming down the road. Him, turning round to look at me. Me, sticking my middle finger up at him.

I slumped down next to Dad, folded my arms and glared at Granddad. He looked at me, winked at my Dad, and said, 'Young people. They have their ways, I suppose. Why don't us men go for a walk before we eat dinner?'

'Perfect,' I thought. 'This is the right time. As soon as Mum leaves, it all goes down his pants.' Jani didn't notice the men leaving, or me glaring at him. I waited for a bit, and said, 'So, what's this then, you sack of farts?'

'What's what?' Jani said, without taking his eyes off his mobile phone.

'Put that thing down and talk to me now or…' I looked at the chicken bowl and warned him . . . 'you're going to need a lot of ice.'

Jani put the phone in his pocket, looked sheepishly at me, and said, 'It's not what you think.'

'What's not what I think?' I asked. 'I don't want to marry you,' Jani said.

Mum stood by the door pretending not to be listening.
'Who the hell wants to marry *you?*' I asked.

'I mean, I didn't come here to marry you,' Jani said.

'Why did you come at all, you idiot?' I said. 'You know I hate you.'

'Me Dad said he would buy me a new bike if I just came with him.'

Mum burst out laughing. I went up to Jani and whispered things no Mum should hear. His freckly face went bright red.

When the men returned, Mum and I looked at each other and couldn't stop laughing. Granddad looked shrivelled up and sunken. I could tell he felt really let down and humiliated in front of Jani's Dad. However, when he saw how happy we all were, he straightened and nudged my Dad, with a *seeItoldyouso* type of a nudge. My Dad frowned and rubbed his hand over his head not knowing which way to look. Jani's Dad twiddled with some prayer beads and said aloud, 'AllahOSomething'.

The men sat down, and Mum and I walked out of the living room. They ate quietly. Mum and I collected a few things from the kitchen and came back. As we got to the front room, we heard Jani's father say, 'Well, don, 'Well, son, are you happy with the decision?'

Mum and I stopped where we were. There was a pause, and Jani's father said a bit louder, 'Put that thing away. I'm talking to you.'

'What's up, Dad?' Jani stammered.

'Are you happy with our choice?' Jani's Dad asked.

'Yeah, but make sure I get an extended guarantee,' Jani said.

'Guarantee!' Jani's Dad said.

'I want to make sure it's as good uphill as it is down,' Jani said.

'Up. Down!' Jani's father exclaimed.

'Don't want me gears knackering up, Da . . .' Jani stopped mid-sentence with a gasp.

Mum stayed where she was but I strode back into the room, and said, 'Uncle, he's only here for a bicycle. It's cheaper than a bride.' And then I walked back out again, grabbed Mum's hand and we went into the kitchen. We shut the door after us and had a really good *mumdaughter* laugh.

We were wiping our eyes when the front door slammed shut. We looked at each other and Dad came into the kitchen. He had the biggest grin on him I have ever seen. He walked past us, opened the fridge, pulled out a can of beer and went back into the living room, shaking his head incredulously.

After everyone had left, Mum asked me if I wanted to go shopping with her and Dad. I said I didn't, and slumped on the settee instead and didn't wake up again until they came back home. When I opened the door, Mum walked right past me as though I wasn't there. Dad was singing, a newspaper under his armpit. It fell on the floor. It was the *Boarhead Evening News*. The front page had a smiling Alex Ferguson, the Man U manager, on it. Now was my time, I thought.

I picked up the newspaper, hugged Dad, and asked, 'Can we all please go to Pakistan for Christmas this year?'

Mum gave me a look that frightened me. She went like this once a year. Near Christmas.

'I don't have any time this year,' Dad said, avoiding eye contact with me.

'My friend Laila's going with her family, I could go with her and visit your village and meet the relatives I have never seen.'

'No,' Dad stood up and looked out of the window.

'Why can't I go, Dad?' I asked. 'I was born there, why can't I go for a visit?'

He didn't turn around.

'Mum?'

She remained silent. Her face was ghostly white.

'If it's money, I'll pay you back when I grow up,' I said.

I waited for either of them to say something back, but they just looked through each other. Leaving them to their stares, I went up to my bedroom.

By the time I got there, Mum and Dad were shouting at each other. *It* was back. But this time it was different. I shut my door, but I could still hear them arguing. I couldn't work out what they were saying to each other, only that my name kept coming up.

Mum and Dad were always arguing, ever since the day I asked if I could go to Pakistan. If they knew I was around, they would go silent and behave as though they were strangers. I could see my family falling apart. I wanted to ask them why they were destroying each other. I had rights, didn't I? I was a part of this family, wasn't I? I had a say about us staying together, didn't I? I loved them and I knew, deep down, they loved each other. What was so bad that they were ripping each other apart? Why couldn't they just kiss and make up, like they used to? But I was not a part of this grown-up world and they made sure I was kept out.

Mum and Dad were not fighting like Mums and Dads fight: about shopping, cleaning, going out or watching television. Mine were fighting about something they did not want me to know. And I could tell it was to do with me. Maybe because I was a Muslim now? I asked Mum this very question when she was sitting alone in the kitchen dicing the onions, over and over again. A pot of daal was boiling on the cooker behind her.

She put the knife down on the table, wiped her hands, leaned over and kissed me on the forehead. She stood up, lifted the lid off the pan, stirred the daal and switched the extractor on. It burst noisily into life, sucking the steam up into its innards.

Mum's kiss was a dry, empty kiss. Her lips had hardly touched me. The kiss fell off my forehead as soon as she turned around.

After putting the lid back on the pan, she picked up a bulb of garlic, sat back down, placed the garlic next to her and started chopping the diced onions again.

'You know I love you and Dad, Mum,' I said. 'Can't you two just make it up like you used to?'

She didn't answer. I didn't think she would. I started peeling the garlic.

Placing the peeled garlic in front of her, I said, 'It doesn't matter, I won't go to Pakistan. I just asked. It's not that important.'

Mum stopped chopping and looked at me. The knife still in her hand. Its blade up. Her eyes suddenly filled with tears. They trembled on the edges of her eyelids. One of them slid down her face. She flicked it off her cheek.

'Mum, please,' I called out.

She wiped her eyes with the back of her hand, then pursed her lips and shook her head.

'Is it because of Jake?' I asked. 'I need to know what's going on, Mum. He's not my boyfriend, Mum. Honest. I'm not like that. He's my mate. You know he's from WTM. Besides he's not my type.'

I laughed falsely and waited for Mum to smile. Instead, she just looked through me and I said, 'I wouldn't do anything to hurt you. Honest, Mum. I love you.'

Her grip tightened on the knife. Her lips quivered. And then the front door slammed shut. My Dad was back.

He came straight into the kitchen. 'Hi, Dad,' I said.

He kissed me on the head and put his sandwich box on the table next to me. Mum and Dad didn't look at each other. Mum scraped the onions onto a plate and chopped up the garlic I'd peeled. Dad took a can of beer out of the fridge. He stirred the daal, and as he stood there drinking his beer, I looked at him and tried to find where the lovely cuddly bear of a Dad of mine had gone.

'Daal, again,' he said.

Mum dug the knife into the board, and said, 'At least you can eat...'

'Will you never let go?' Dad asked.

I ran upstairs and sat on my bed. After a while, I got up and opened the window. A cold wind came rushing in. I stuck my head outside. It was a bright day. George's dog was sitting in its usual place, staring at a magpie, sitting on the dance mat. George was looking through some CDs.

Downstairs they were shouting at each other. I heard the muffled words.

Pakistan.

Why?

George put a CD in his ghetto blaster. The noise of the music drowned Mum and Dad out. I left my collapsing world downstairs and thought back. I could not remember a time they went out together, other than to the supermarket. Maybe I could give them some time together. They could go out for a bit. Mum was always wandering through the house, like a ghost, looking for something and Dad was always glued to the television, avoiding the ghost. Why hadn't I seen it before? I cursed myself. They were both spending all their time together running away from each other.

I lost track of time, and only came back to my world with a jolt when George turned the music off.

Dad was walking out of the gate.

Just then, I saw Shamshad coming towards our house. There was a knock on our door. I ran down to tell her to get lost, but Mum got the door. Mum had a glass of juice in her hand.

'I just wanted to tell you that that half-caste daughter of yours is going out with Jake Smith,' Shamshad said.

She sniggered and left.

'She's lying, Mum. Lying!' I cried. And then I shouted after Shamshad, 'I hope you die!'

Mum said in a strangely calm way, 'You shouldn't say things like that about her...'

'She's just evil,' I hissed. 'Evil!'

Mum said coldly, 'And *you* should not wish evil things onto others. There is much you don't understand. You are young. What she did might be bad but she was not born bad. No one is...'

'What are you taking her side for?' I interrupted rudely. 'Who do you think you are?'

'I will not be spoken to like this,' Mum replied sternly. 'Go to your room, right now, and think about what you just did.'

'What did I do?'

'Go upstairs!'

'You're on her side against me,' I said, pointing to Shamshad, who was standing on the pavement enjoying every moment of my misery. 'What is it, Mum? Didn't you want me? Did you want a boy?'

At that, my angry Mum once more turned into a ghost of a Mum. I slammed the door shut. I didn't know what I had said that was so bad. *It* was back. She took deep slow breaths. The sides of her mouth were twitching like she was chewing on something. She began to sweat. She raised her hand to hit me and then she looked at her open palm. She had never hit me before. I screamed, 'Mum, you're scaring me!'

Her hand froze in the air. She gazed at me with a blank look in her eyes, then turned and walked up the stairs, mumbling something under her breath. I went after her, but by the time I got to the top of the stairs, she had already shut the door and locked herself in her room.

'Why do you have to say things that you know will hurt her, I cursed myself in my head.

I banged on the door, begging her to let me in. I wanted to tell her how sorry I was and that I would never do it again. What she did today, she had never done before and I knew it was no good knocking; she would never open the door when she was in one of her freaky silences. Not for me, not for my Dad; no one could enter into this world of hers.

Sometimes she went into this world, leaving the door ajar. I would walk past her bedroom, as quietly as I could, and peep inside. She would just sit there, on the floor, next to her bed, clutching her little box, which I had seen her hiding under the floorboards. Sometimes she would let out a scream. A terrifying scream that came from deep inside her, in a voice that did not sound like hers. She would scream and scream until she went hoarse. She would just as quickly stop screaming and start swaying to and fro with her box. Her face drained of colour. Her hair covering her face. Her eyes so empty. I always thought that if I ever witnessed an animal being killed, it would make a sound like my Mum, moments before its throat was slit.

I was about to leave when I heard her walking around in her bedroom. I heard her unlock the door. I stopped. The door creaked open. I heard her walking in the room again. I turned around and she was sitting exactly where she always did when she went into one of these moods. She took a deep breath, and said without looking at me, 'I have cooked for you.'

'I'm not hungry, Mum.'

'I have cooked for you.'

'I told you, I'm not hungry.'

'I have cooked for you.'

The front door slammed shut. Dad was back.

'Dad, come upstairs now. It's Mum!' I called out to him. He didn't answer.

'Mum, please, you're frightening me.'

I went into the room and brushed the hair off her face. Her eyes were bloodshot.

I ran downstairs. Dad was flicking through the TV channels.

'There's something wrong with Mum, Dad.' He pursed his lips and nodded. 'Dad!' I shouted.

He turned away from me, clenched his fist, cracking his fingers. There was a strange wall between us. His mobile phone buzzed into life. 'Answer me, Dad,' I said, grabbing the phone off the sideboard. Switching it off, I asked, 'What's wrong with Mum?'

'Nothing,' he sighed.

'I am not a child any more, Dad. Tell me now. Come upstairs and look at her - and then tell me there's nothing wrong with her.'

Dad kept quiet.

'There's nothing proper about this house, is there?'

I waited for him to answer. He sat down. I cried, 'Please Dad, call a doctor or something. Mum needs help.'

'She'll be alright, sweetheart.' His voice was heavy.

'Come upstairs with me, please Dad.'

He shrugged dully, just as I had expected. He never did go to Mum when she was like this. It was like they didn't know each other.

I ran back upstairs to Mum. She was hiding the box. I waited for her to finish hiding it before going in.

'Mum, I'm really, really scared.'

'It will have gone cold now,' she said, tying her hair.

I went into my room and thought aloud, 'Well Kiran, you're going to find out what's in that little box.'

They were arguing again. This time they were not shouting. I went into the living room. They were sitting opposite each other, across the coffee table: the television was off, the curtains shut. They looked at me as I walked in and it was a look I didn't want.

'Sit down, Kiran,' Dad said.

I stood there, looking at them. Their eyes were bloodshot, their faces sunken. Mum's hair was all curled up and the tip of her nose was red. Dad sat on the edge of the settee, hands locked together, chin on his hands, eyes fixed on me.

'We need to talk to you,' he said.

'I don't want to hear what you're about to say to me,' I replied. A shiver ran down my neck. He went quiet. I looked at Mum, and asked, 'Mum?'

A tear fell out of her eye. It landed on the back of her bony hand. She rubbed it into her skin with her other hand.

'You love each other, right, Dad?' I asked. 'Right, Mum?'

'Sometimes things are just not meant to be, Kiran,' Dad said. 'Even when two people love each other, they can lose what they had.'

My legs were giving way. I sat on a chair beside the coffee table. 'I just want my family,' I said.

Then, 'Is it because I put this on?' I said, ripping off my hijab. I threw it towards the television.

Mum stood up, picked up my hijab and put it back on my head with shaking hands.

'At least tell me why?' I pleaded.

No one spoke for what seemed like an eternity. And then Dad said, 'Some things can't be explained, Kiran.'

'Are you really breaking up? My family? You two? Really, really breaking it all up?' I stood up and went into the kitchen. Two suitcases were packed and a few boxes were stacked on top of each other. I kicked the suitcases, went back into the living room, and shouted at Dad, 'You're really, really leaving, aren't you?'

'It's for the best, Kiran,' Mum said.

'And what's going to happen to me?'

'You're coming with me,' Dad said. 'We'll live at your Granddad's for a while and then get our own place. Everything will work out just fine. You'll see.'

'Just fine,' I thought. 'Yep. I'll be just fine. All my dreams destroyed.

'Everything shattered. Just fine! That's what you call it. Yep.

'Do you think I'm going to just leave Mum on her own?' I cried. 'Do you?'

Mum stood up and hugged me. She was trembling. She whispered into my ear, with a faded voice, 'You're staying with me, love, always staying with me.'

'Your Mum's going to be off work for a while,' Dad said, standing up, and telling her: 'I'll send you some money every week and don't worry about any of the bills…'

I ran towards him and tried to punch Dad in the chest, saying, 'How can you be so calm? How can you?' He held my wrists in his strong, rough hands, hugged me and cried. Then he pulled away from me, kissed me on the cheeks and walked out of the living room.

At first, I didn't believe Mum and Dad would really break up. Even when he had left, I thought Dad was going to come back and slobber in front of the television. I thought Mum would just snap out of her silences. But Dad didn't come back and Mum went more and more silent. Dad came round each Friday evening and handed me an envelope, standing on the front doorstep. We talked about things that didn't matter, and he left for a week. When he came round, Mum hid somewhere in the house. When he left, Mum didn't really come out, she just changed rooms. Most of the time, she was in her room, mumbling to herself, words that I didn't understand; we were a broken family, whose reasons for breaking up didn't make sense.

I gave the envelopes with the money to Mum. She put them on top of each other in a cupboard in the kitchen.

Dad took care of the bills, and I did the shopping, cooking, and cleaning. Mum withered away.

I spent endless hours walking around the house trying to work out why my family had broken up. Thinking about ways I could get it back together again. I thought back over all the arguments I had heard Mum and Dad having, and cursed myself for not listening to what they were saying to each other. I recalled the fragments of the loaded words that shattered my family: *Pakistan*

Whatever it was, it had to do with me. That much was clear. I was born in Pakistan, in my Dad's village, when Mum and Dad went out there in 1996. That much I knew. I came to England when I was just a few months old. But I never went back again. Maybe we just couldn't afford it? I don't know. Maybe I was just an accident, not what they wanted. Maybe, they wanted a boy and I turned up and I was horrible. But Mum and Dad had always loved me. I never felt unwanted in this family. The day of the break-up had been the first birthday Dad forgot about. He never forgot my birthday even though he usually forgot his own.

And those terrible cries of Mum, calling out to God. The screams that pierced through the house when they argued. I remembered that when they argued, it was always close to Christmas. They shouted at each other until Mum hid in her room. Dad drank and watched football. I used to put my headphones on and blot them out. That's what grown-ups did, I thought. It was all normal. A happy family arguing with itself.

I blamed myself over and over again. Why didn't I see there was something terribly wrong with my family? Maybe Mum or Dad was having an affair with someone else? I couldn't believe this. They never went out other than for shopping. And in all their arguments, I didn't once hear a word that might have meant this could possibly be the end of my family. One thing I was certain about though: somehow I was at the centre of it all. And as that was the case, I was going to find out what it was and get Mum and Dad back together again.

I had to discover what it was that Mum kept hidden under the floorboards. Whatever it might be, I would find an answer in there. Mum might kill me, but I didn't care. I had to know. The only problem was, Mum never left the house when I was at home.

At school, I avoided everyone but Laila. Jake came up to me a few times, looking all apologetic and wanting to talk, but I gave him the cold shoulder and he kept his distance. It was difficult avoiding Shamshad, though. She often blocked my path after school, saying things like, 'Half-caste families, they're not proper. They always break up.' She didn't frighten me any more, though. She just hurt me. I always kept my head high and walked past her, and then forgot her. I needed to be home. To make sure Mum was OK.

Time went by so quickly. I carried on doing all the housework and shopping. Laila came round at the weekends. Mum would come out of her bedroom when Laila was around, nod to her, and then go back into her room again.

When Laila came round, she not only helped me to clean up but also helped me to read the Quran. I looked forward to Laila's visits. In my new mad world, she made me feel I belonged to something. We prayed together and then chatted about her new favourite subjects: *The X Factor* and boys.

A week before the Christmas holidays, Laila went to Pakistan.

The first snow of the winter fell the week after she left. I saw it falling through my bedroom window. I watched it fall on the rooftops, watched it fall on children throwing snowballs at each other, and watched it cover the cars and hedges. I remembered how Dad used to make me a snowman. He built the best snowman on the street. Even if the snowman was much thinner than he was, and even if it was the only one in East Boarhead with a cucumber for a nose, it was still the best. I fell asleep dreaming of my snowman.

Shamshad

It was bin day, and Karen's Dad was going to pass our street. I had my camera ready. It was charged and waiting on the kitchen table. I'd been meaning to take a photograph of his big, fat ugly face driving the rubbish truck. Our bins are at the back of our house. We place them outside our back gate, in a small alley, and they are taken from there. It was collection day for the black bins. But as no one could remember which day was for the green, the brown or the black, everyone followed whoever got theirs out first. Sometimes it meant most people got it wrong, and if this happened with the green ones, into which the food was meant to go, it didn't half smell, especially in the summer.

The two-legged *majja,* the buffaloes, were out. The short round Mrs Khan, our neighbour, with her big, gold earrings was nattering to two others. The *paan*-chewing Janat Choudry, with her hennaed hair and bell-shaped earrings, bigger than those of Mrs Khan, was shaking her head at the third buffalo: Asmat Jaan. She had a moustache bigger then her husband's, and was always sneaking out for a smoke.

It was really cold. I had my mittens on, but it made little difference. The buffaloes were standing close to each other. This meant there was some really juicy gossip going round otherwise they would be talking to each other from over their fences. Pulling my bin behind me, I got close enough to hear.

'Left that *goree*, his white woman, didn't he?' Mrs Khan said, nodding to the bleeping of the rubbish truck, which was somewhere on the other side, next to the houses that backed onto ours.

'Who?' Janat Choudry asked, with a puzzled wrinkly look.

'Ghanzanfer's son, who lives with that white woman in West Boarhead.'

Asmat Jaan adjusted her *dupatta* across her breasts, and said, 'They never stay with their white women.'

'Nah,' Mrs Khan said.

'But they can't keep their hands off them either, can they?' Janat Choudry said, lifting the lid off her bin. She spat into the bin, and added, '*Goreyaan*!'

'He's going to Pakistan,' Mrs Khan said.

'Who?' Janat Choudry asked, putting another *paan* into her mouth.

'Ghanzanfer's son,' Asmat Jaan said, lighting a cigarette. 'He's coming back next week with another woman.'

'They always do,' Mrs Khan said, untangling an earring, which had got stuck in her hair.

'When their *goreyaan*, their white women, kick them out,' Janat Choudry said, chewing her *paan*.

Blowing smoke out of her nostrils, Asmat Jaan said, 'They have the luck of fate, the *goreyaan*,' and she laughed.

'They do. That they do. And we are stuck with ours,' Mrs Khan said.

The buffaloes laughed.

I asked loudly, 'Any news you can share with me, aunties?'

Asmat Jaan let her cigarette drop to the ground, and said, 'It's going to be cold this year.'

'You should wrap yourself up, young girl,' Mrs Khan said. 'Look after yourself properly,' Janat Choudry said.

'And you're out without even your jumper,' I said.

'Nothing'll happen to us old buffaloes,' Asmat Jaan said.

The old women laughed as I walked back into the house, clenching my fists with joy. I washed my hands and could see the words flying off on my Facebook: *Karen's Dad is off to Pakistan to get another wife. Hey Karen, your Dad really is Lucky!! He's got a new Mum for you in Pakistan. He's bringing her back next week. Wanna see pictures. Lol.*

After I put these words up on my Facebook status, I waited for Likes. I waited and waited, but not one Liked my post. I expected lots of LOLs and hahahas. But nothing. Eventually Aisha wrote: *omg. Sad.*

I don't know why Aisha's word *sad* so upset me. But I suddenly felt what I had done was really, really bad. I was bad. Always showing off. A big bad bully. It was me who was the sad case.

'*Allahjee*, help.' I cried. 'Please, God, forgive me.'

I went back and started writing another status. I wanted to say sorry, but I just couldn't do it. I would look even more stupid than I was.

Kiran

It was past 11 o'clock in the morning when I woke up the next day. I could hear Mum in the bathroom. I put on my dressing gown and went downstairs. There was a letter on the front door mat. It was from Dad. It said: *Going to Pakistan tomorrow. Will tell you all about it when I come back. My number is on the back of this paper.*

I opened the front door. Footprints in the snow led from the door to the garden. The cold wrapped itself around me as I slipped into my shoes and stepped out. There was a snowman in the garden. Just like Dad used to make. With tomato eyes and a cucumber nose. I snatched my eyes off the snowman; it was already making me feel sad and angry.

I shut the door and pinned the letter from Dad onto a board near the cloak rack.

'Come upstairs now,' Mum called.

'Dad's gone to Pakistan,' I shouted back.

Mum went silent for a moment and then said, 'And bring lots of bin liners with you.'

I went into the kitchen. It was a mess. The sink was full of unwashed dishes. Two pots, half-filled with food and with their lids off, were on the cooker. An overflowing ashtray, full of half-smoked cigarettes, was on the worktop next to a dirty serving spoon.

I opened the drawer in which the bin liners were kept and took the whole bundle with me before I went up to Mum. The room stank of cigarettes. It was damp and cold. The curtains were drawn and her bedside lamp was on. She was standing in front of her open wardrobe, staring at her clothes.

She unfolded a bin bag, fanned it open, and gave it to me to hold. And then one after the other, she took her dresses out of the wardrobe and dumped them into the bag.

'Going to buy some new ones at last, Mum?' I asked.

She ignored me. When the bag was full, she said, 'Take it downstairs.'

I did. When I came back, she had filled another one and handed it to me. I took that down as well. The next time I went back up, she was on the phone, saying, 'George the curry club is dead. Finished. Tell the others.'

I left Mum and ran downstairs into the living room, half expecting to see Dad sitting there, glued to the television. The silence of the room boomed around my ears.

Mum came downstairs with a bin liner in her hand and walked out of the house. She came back a few moments later, picked up another two and as she was leaving, I asked, 'What you going to do with them, Mum?'

Without stopping to look at me, she mumbled, 'Someone else may like them,' and left, leaving the door open behind her. I got up and stood in the doorway, watching her throw the bags into the back of the car and drive away.

I don't know where the rest of the day went. She just smoked and got rid of most of her things.

I couldn't remember the last time I had seen her eat anything so I went into the kitchen and made her a cheese and cucumber sandwich. She was sitting at the top of the stairs, looking down at me with empty eyes.

Walking up the stairs I held the sandwich up to her and said, 'Here Mum, please eat this.'

She ignored me. Putting the sandwich next to her I said, 'Please, Mum, talk to me.'

'The bins need putting out,' was all she said.

'Damn you, Mum,' I thought, getting up. 'How long's this going to go on for?'

I ran downstairs and went into the living room, slamming the door shut after me.

Just then I got a text from Laila: *Is it true?* I messaged her back: *What?*

Go to FB, she texted.

I rushed to my bedroom; Mum was still sitting on the stairs. I logged onto Facebook.

I went to Shamshad's FB profile and read what she had written. 'And damn *you*, Shamshad,' I cursed

I stomped downstairs, fetched the piece of paper with Dad's number from the noticeboard and dialled. Waiting for the line to connect, I looked at the time. It was 8 p.m. I tried to work out what time it would be in Pakistan but gave up. I didn't care if he was asleep or awake.

After a little while, a long tone started ringing. When he answered, I said, 'Dad?'

'Kiran, sweetie, is everything alright?' he said, sleepily.

'You tell me,' I said bitterly.

Dad went silent.

'You couldn't wait, eh.

'You're done with the *goree*, have you? Not good enough for you now, eh. Got yourself a proper one, eh.'

'Kiran, Kiran. Listen,' Dad interrupted.

I didn't let him finish, 'So you left your half-caste kid, eh. Not proper, am I, eh.'

'It's not like that, I love…'

'And that white woman you walked out on? Every day a bit of her dies.' The phone was stuck to my hand. I was sweating all over. I didn't hear Mum coming. She sat on the last step, close to me.

'What's the matter?' she asked.

'It's Mr Lucky. I'm talking to him in Pakistan.'

Mum went quiet. I said to Dad, 'Go on then, what've you got to tell me?'

'It's not what you think, Kiran. You need to know everything. And when I get back, I promise you'll know. I'm doing this for you, Kiran.'

That just did it. I let rip down the telephone, 'I hate you and never want to see you again!' I said, slamming the receiver down.

Turning to Mum, I said, 'He's got another woman!'

She threw her shoulders up and asked, 'What else did he say?'

'"It's not what you think, Kiran. You need to know everything. And when I get back, I promise you'll know", I said, mimicking Dad. '"I'm doing it for you, *Kiran*".

'You had to find out someday,' Mum said.

She went back to her bedroom. Her words were banging against the inside of my head. What did I have to know? Is this how it happens? Mums and Dads break up, just like that. Dads go off to get married again. Just like that.

The telephone rang. It was Dad.

'There's a lot you need to know. I'm back next week, and I promise I'll tell you everything. Everything! No more secrets,' he said. After a pause, he asked, 'Can I speak to your Mum?'

'You've really got a nerve, haven't you? Don't you dare come to our house! Do you hear?' I said, once more slamming the telephone down.

Shamshad

What should have been another boring day, with me coming home from mosque school, Mum oblivious of my arriving as she nattered on Skype, cursing some villager about her goats or the condition of her fields, became a day when my world just collapsed. Everything was a lie.

When I walked in, Mum was on Skype, but she was not talking, just staring at the screen. This was a first. She then glanced at my reflection in a mirror that sat on top of a chest of drawers in the room. Her eyes moved from the computer screen to me, and then back to the computer again.

'Is everything OK, Mum?' I asked, waiting for her to do one of her outbursts or shut the door in my face. But she just flicked another look at me and went back to staring at the computer.

When I got a bit closer, I felt a jolt go through my body. There was no mistaking who she was looking at. Karen's father, Lucky, was standing next to Mum's goat herder, a hard-faced, dark woman. They were looking into the camera. When I got a bit closer, Karen's Dad's face tilted towards the woman. It looked like the screen was stuck. The woman put her hand on her mouth.

'What's up, Mum?' I asked.

The woman on the screen let out a wail. The connection was bad, cutting her voice.

A tear rolled down Mum's face.

The front door opened and shut with a loud bang. The glass chandelier hanging in the middle of the room jingled. Dad was home. And Mum hadn't turned the computer off. I didn't want all hell breaking loose.

'What're you doing, Mum?' I whispered, moving my hand forward to turn the computer off. 'He's home.'

Mum grabbed my hand and stopped me from turning the computer off.

She was looking at me in the mirror. There was no fear in her eyes.

In the mirror, I saw the door opening behind me. Dad was taken aback when he saw us together, standing in front of the computer. When he realised who we were looking at, his eyes narrowed. His face tightened and he hissed through his nose. I stepped away from Mum, and stood pressing my back against the wall, underneath a picture frame with the word 'Allah' written in golden Arabic lettering.

Dad looked at me and pointed to the door. I turned to leave, but Mum grabbed me by the wrist, holding me tightly. Dad's eyes burned down on Mum's hand.

First he took off his black winter coat and threw it on the sofa, showering the carpet with snow. Then he unplugged the computer from the mains.

'She has to know,' Mum said, loosening her grip.

'You dare defy me,' Dad said, taking off his shoe. Mum just stood there. Her head unbowed.

'Oh, Dad, no!' I pleaded.

'Lower your head, woman,' Dad said, stepping towards us, the shoe in his hand raised.

*

Mum let go of my hand.

'Dad, please', I repeated, 'it's all my fault.'

'What have we done?' Mum said, looking Dad in the face.

When Dad brought his hand down to hit Mum, I just snapped and ran at him screaming, 'You will never do that again! It's a crime against Allah and it's a crime against Mum and it's a crime against me.'

His arm froze mid-air, shoe in hand.

'Never as long as I live, Dad, never!' I screamed.

Mum put her arm around me and said, 'We have lied to Shamshad. We have lied to God.'

Dad dropped the shoe. He was so shocked he stumbled backwards. Regaining his posture, he let out a stream of obscenities. He no longer looked terrifying. Just pathetic. I put my hands on my ears and ran out of the room as their words lashed each other.

'You will never hit me again!'

'It is all your fault! You're barren!'

'You're seedless!'

'Leave this house now, woman!'

'It is mine!'

Their words chased me all the way up the stairs. I shut my bedroom door. I could still hear them, but the words were muffled now. I wanted to go back and ask them to tell me what I had done to bring this down on us. I waited for a moment and then opened my door to go down.

Mum was shouting at Dad, 'Is there a bigger crime than what we have committed?'

I turned around and went back into my room. The snow had stopped. The world was frozen. I picked up my headphones and put them on my head. With my shoes still on, I jumped onto my bed, pressed the play button on my iPod and sang loudly along with Lady Gaga.

When the song finished, I took off the headphones and threw them against the door. The war downstairs was still raging. I turned my head and buried my face into my pillow, cried and fell asleep.

I woke sometime later. My curtains were drawn. It was past 2 a.m. A cat was wailing somewhere, like a lost baby crying for its mother. Popping my head behind the curtains, I half expected the cat to be sat outside my window. There was no cat, only a world drowning in falling snow.

My stomach rumbled a hungry rumble. I put on my bedside lamp. There was a glass of milk next to it, along with some rotis wrapped in a cloth. Mum had left me a snack. I woke up late the next morning, and stayed in bed a bit longer, just to make sure Dad would have left for work, all the while trying to make sense of the words Mum and Dad had hurled at each other.

When I opened my bedroom door, the house was filled with the smell of roasting parathas and buttered rotis. I didn't bother cleaning my teeth or washing my face and went down.

Dad was still at home. He was sitting on his own, in the living room, staring at the wall in front of him. The door was wide open. His coat was still where he had left it. His shoe was where it had fallen the night before.

Mum called me from the kitchen, 'Shamshad, come here.'

'I'm late for the mosque, Mum.'

‘Come here,’ she insisted.

I said, ‘I’m not hungry Mum, honest.’

My stomach grumbled in protest as I walked into the kitchen, swallowing a hard lump in my throat. Mum smiled at me. She was holding an egg in her hand. She cracked it on the side of the frying pan and the contents of the egg sizzled in the hot oil.

Putting the fried egg onto a small plate, Mum placed it next to the paratha and a glass of orange juice. She stood there looking at me. I pulled the food towards me, broke a piece of paratha and dipped it into the yolk. The yolk broke and dribbled into the white. I ate in silence, drank my juice and walked out of the kitchen.

Dad stole a look at me as I went past the front living room and out of the door.

In the mosque, I didn’t help with teaching the younger ones like I usually did. I squatted against a wall and stared down at the open pages of the Quran. I tried to remember the sounds in my head, the sounds of a language I didn’t understand, but which was being recited by little children all around the room.

I kept hearing Mum and Dad’s words going round and round in my head: *Is there a bigger crime than what we have committed? Barren. Seedless.*

What had they done? ‘Whatever else it is, girl,’ I thought, ‘you are not wanted. And you’re not a kid. You know what they’re talking about.

‘Stop now’, I said to the thoughts inside my head. They were hurting me. I didn’t want to know. I chased them away by reciting the Quran, but they clung on.

I would have stayed at the mosque much longer, but had to leave before the start of the boys’ session. I walked home as slowly as I could, dragging my feet through the slush, oblivious to the falling snow. A snow flake went into my eye, but I was burning up inside.

I thought about running away from home. But where would I go? I was not only hated at home, but I knew, deep down, I was hated by everyone, and even those who said they were my friends were just frightened of me. My mobile rang a few times. It was Mum. It had to be her. I didn't reply. When I got on our road, Mum was standing outside on the street, looking in my direction. She was wearing her white cardigan, which she had knitted herself. She also had on her black shawl, which was draped across her shoulders. It was peppered with white dots.

When I was close enough to hear, she smiled and said, 'You are a little late, my daughter.'

Vapour came out of Mum's mouth as she spoke.

When she said this, I stopped in my tracks. I just melted inside. I wanted to scream, 'Why have you never called me daughter before?' but instead I kept quiet and glared at her.

A cracked line of red ran through the whites of her eyes.

Something rumbled on the roof of our house. Suddenly an avalanche of snow crashed to the ground.

She stepped forward, wiped the snow off my hijab and said, 'I was just worried.'

I said, 'Sorry!'

Mum's hand slid down my arm and brushed against mine. I began to feel really shaky inside. I thought she was going to hug me. I wanted so much for her to hug me and tell me what was going on. To make me feel we were a proper family, just for once, rather than what we really were, two people living in different prisons in the same house.

Mum held my hand, and said, 'I've cooked your favourite, *koftay*.'

'I don't want *koftay*,' I thought, 'I just want a hug.'

Snatching my hand from her, I went into the house. The first thing I saw was a school photograph of me from the infant's school. I was taken aback. A photograph in my house and of me!

Dad was still sitting on his own in the living room, was still staring at the wall.

Mum shut the door behind me and said softly, 'And I have lived behind hidden feelings for long enough.'

I walked straight into the kitchen, brushed the snow off my coat and hung it on the back of a chair. There were more, newer photographs on the walls. There was one of me and Mum, standing outside our house. Steam from a pot on the cooker was being devoured by the extractor, and the air was filled with the scent of cooked daal. Mum came in after me, lifted the lid off the pan and turned the gas off. She chopped some fresh *dhania*, some coriander, and sprinkled it over the daal in the pan.

Putting her nose close to the rising steam, she inhaled, and said, 'The scent of the daal just after the *dhania* goes in always reminds me of the fall of the rain on the dry summer soil of my village.'

I gritted my teeth, unsure of what to say. If I could have, I would have said, 'Damn your village.' But I said nothing.

Now that I was inside the warmth of our house, I felt cold. After putting the lid back on the pan, Mum took a rolling pin out of a drawer. She rolled a ball out of some freshly made dough, dipped her hand into a bowl of flour, sprinkled it on the worktop, and rolling a roti out said, 'Make some salad, daughter.'

Her voice was soft. A voice I had not heard before. 'Just tell me what's going on, Mum,' I thought. 'Or whoever you are, just tell me.' But once again, I kept quiet. I got up, stood on the other side of the sink, close to where she was and started preparing the salad.

The floorboards of Dad's bedroom, above the kitchen, announced his arrival into his bedroom. Mum looked up, looked at me and let out a little laugh while placing the rolled roti onto the hot *tava*, a hotplate, which had been placed on the cooker. She flipped it over after a few moments, then lifted the *tava* in her left hand, and with the other hand she placed the roti onto the naked flame. It began to puff up and up. When it was fully inflated, she tapped it on the top and quickly withdrew her hand as steam burst out of the roti. She picked it up and placed it on a cloth.

I made a bed of lettuce leaves. Then chopped the cucumbers and tomatoes and put them onto the lettuce.

Dad was moving about in his room.

After putting the salad plate on the table, I sat back down and watched Mum as she made more rotis. She washed her hands after she had finished the final one. Letting out a deep sigh, she looked at me. Her face was sad again. The wrinkles were back. She was looking through me with her dark eyes. She let out another sigh. A smile had flown in from somewhere and landed on her face. Her eyes were sullen, but they were no longer the ones I had grown up with. These were calm. Her gaze was so intense, as if she had not seen me for a long time. The wrinkles on her brown face were gone again.

'What is it, Mum?' I asked, unwrapping the rotis from the cloth.

Mum put some daal into two bowls, put one in front of me and one in front of her. She then placed a plate of *koftay*, meat-balls, in front of me and said, sitting down, 'You've grown up so quickly.'

The scent of fresh coriander rose up in the steam from the daal on my plate.

'I'm fourteen, Mum,' I said, dipping a piece of roti into the daal and putting it into my mouth. I didn't feel like eating.

Running a finger over the lettuce in the salad plate, Mum said, 'I don't know where it went.'

'What?' I asked.

'Time.'

'I'm not that old,' I said.

'You're all grown up, a woman.'

Nodding to the ceiling, I let out my first little laugh in days. 'He's not thinking about a goat herder for me, is he?'

I knew I shouldn't have said what I said, even as I said it. But it was too late.

Mum's cheeks sank. The pupils in her eyes shrank. Colour left her face. And with another sigh she was back, saying, 'He will never hurt us again.'

My throat dried. The roti in my mouth refused to go down.

Dad dropped something upstairs. He took a few heavy steps, and then took a few more and slumped onto his bed.

I felt cold all of a sudden, a chill that went deep into my bones.

Mum stood up, came round the table and kissed me on each eye. She whispered, 'No one will ever hurt my angel. No one.'

She sat down next to me, broke a piece of roti, dipped it in my daal and put it in my mouth, saying, 'Shush, now. Eat.'

I was trembling.

She stroked my cheek. The lump in my throat became bigger. Drier. I chewed slowly. Scared of the volcano rising inside of me.

After a few moments in which the clock ticked, in which a blaring police siren from somewhere close by invaded the room, in which someone laughed in the back alley, in which music came in through the walls of the house next door, Mum took my hands in hers, held them tightly, and said, 'You need to know everything. Soon. But I've not been a good mother, have I?'

'It's alright, Mum.'

'I wish I was…'

'You're my Mum, and that's all that matters.'

'I wish I was . . .' she said again.

Kiran

That night after talking to Dad in Pakistan I kept tossing and turning in bed, falling in and out of sleep, cursing him in my dreams, 'Lucky, I hope you die.' In the morning when Mum came downstairs, she was dressed in her long, black winter coat. Her hair was tucked into a woolly hat and she was wearing her red gloves. She opened the door and left.

She didn't tell me where she was going or when she would be back, and I didn't ask her.

I watched her leave the yard and turn left.

I had decided to find out what was under her bed. I didn't really care even if she came back early and caught me in the act; but when I got to her door, I got scared. A chill ran down my back. This small room suddenly felt so big, like a huge, terrifying cave. I could feel her presence. I could smell her.

The quilt on Mum's bed was folded back at the corner from where she'd got out of bed. The rest of it looked as if it hadn't been touched. The main light bulb was fused. I put my hand up her lacy bedside lamp and turned it on. As the light came on, shadows from the moving tassels bounced off a picture of Mum and Dad. It had been taken when they were young. They were standing together yet seemed so far apart. Mum had that lost look in her green eyes. Dad had a *saycheese* type of a smile. Turning away from the picture, I sat down and looked under the bed.

Apart from a few coins, there was nothing else there. There was no place anything could be hidden. Maybe she lifts the bed up and gets under the floorboards that way?' I thought.

I tried to lift the bed up. It didn't budge. I thought of calling Jake, then I looked a bit closer. The carpet was covered in a layer of dust and the corner next to the leg of the bed had fingermarks on it. I touched the carpet there. It moved. It was cut at the point where the leg of the bed sat. I peeled it back. The underlay was also cut. I peeled that back too.

One of the floorboards had a long, thin cut in it. At one end, there was a small hole. I put my finger into the hole and lifted the wood. Blood pumped around my ears. A damp, musky smell came out from under the floorboards. There was nothing there. I put my hand inside and rummaged about. I felt the box and took it out.

I carried it over to the lamp and looked at it. It was a carved brown wooden box similar to the one we had in the kitchen for the tissues. Everyone in Dad's family had one of these. However, unlike the tissue boxes, this one had a lid on it, with a small brass hook.

I brought the box downstairs. My heart was pounding. Why would she hide it? What was in it? For a moment, I felt guilty. This was her secret, secret world and I was rummaging through it. I felt bad. But then I flushed with anger. How dare she hide it from me! I put the box down on the kitchen table and stared at the flowers carved into it. I hoped its little bronze lock would just flip off and the lid open by itself. I waited and waited for the lid to open by itself but it didn't. 'Please open now,' I cried. But it would not.

I wished Laila was here and not in Pakistan. I really, really wanted her now.

'What shall I do, Laila?' I asked aloud.

I saw her face flash through my mind. She was smiling.

'Yes, I'll call him, Laila,' I said to the smiling face in my mind and called Jake.

Waiting for Jake, I sat down on a chair in front of the box and didn't take my eyes off it, half wanting to throw it onto the ground and smash it into pieces and half in terror of what might jump out at me from inside it.

I lost track of time and only came back out of my thoughts when I heard Jake talking outside my house.

Mum was back, I thought. Who else could he be talking to?

I opened the door. Jake was alone, recording a message into his mobile. 'I'm outside her house now. Bye, Laila.'

Before I could ask what he was doing messaging Laila he said, 'I was driving around and we were just chatting when you called.'

I was gob-smacked by the 'we'. But what the hell.

'I borrowed me Dad's car,' Jake said, dangling a set of keys in front of me. 'Bet you didn't know I could drive,' he said nervously.

'Of course I know you can drive, jerk,' I thought. 'I've seen you nick cars.'

For a moment, I forgot about the box. But only for a moment.

I went into the kitchen, and Jake followed me.

‘That,’ I said, pointing to the box. ‘Whatever is in that box…’

‘It’s just a box,’ he said.

‘Mum kept it hidden under her bed.’

‘All Mums and Dads have something hidden under their bed. Mine’s got whiskey . . .’

‘It’s serious, this, Jake.’

‘Sorry, Kiran, I didn’t mean it like that.’

I looked at the box for one last time, then quickly opened it. Inside the box was a dummy, a babygro and a Hi8 camera tape. The dummy was white and the baby grower, a faded blue. I sniffed the baby suit. It smelt of mould. I took the tape out and looked at the word Hi8. I hadn’t seen anything like it before.

Jake gazed at the contents of the box for a while and said, touching the babygro, ‘Its blue. It’s a boy’s.’

I felt numb inside. I picked up the tape, and asked, ’What would play this?’

‘Let’s get it transferred onto a disk,’ Jake said. ‘Andy’s Videos’ll do it.’

‘No,’ I thought. ‘I don’t want to know. I don’t want to see whatever was on it.’

‘When’s your Mum back?’ Jake asked and I shrugged.

‘Come on,’ Jake said. I followed him out of the door.

Andy’s Videos was at the bottom of St. George’s Street, a few minutes’ walk from home. I floated dreamlike to the shop. Jake gave the tape in and an eternity later, we walked out with the tape and a CD. Back home, Jake handed me the CD and the tape. I put the CD into the DVD player.

Holding the remote in my hand, I said, ‘I can’t do this.’

‘Up to you, Kiran.’

I pressed play.

There was Mum showing off her bulging belly, smiling proudly, laughing. She was so beautiful with her golden hair flowing across her face. The screen went blank and there was Mum again. With a baby. Very small. Very pink. Dad was laughing.

After a few minutes of the baby in a basket, the screen went dead again.

When the picture came back, there was Dad with a can of beer in his hand. Mum was filming. He was standing close to the baby. The baby cried.

'Pick him up,' Mum laughed, her voice booming loudly.

Dad took a swig. The screen went blank again and came back. The baby was sitting up on the ground. The screen went blank and remained blank.

'She had a baby before me, Jake,' I said, taking the CD out of the player. My stomach knotted, and I felt my chest caving in. My ears were burning. 'So I have a baby brother,' I thought. Mum's face flashed through my mind. *How dare you keep this from me! How dare you! Where is my brother? What happened to him?*

Though I didn't want to admit it to myself, deep down I knew.

No one said anything for what felt like an eternity. Then the front door opened and shut. Mum was back.

She walked into the kitchen. I heard the sound of breaking glass. She came into the living room a few moments later. Box in hand. She picked up the Hi8 off the coffee table, opened the lid of the box, put the tape into it, shut the lid and turned around to leave.

'I know what's on the tape, Mum.'

Without saying anything, Mum started to walk out of the room.

As she was leaving I demanded, 'Is that it? You've got nothing to say to me? Nothing? You liar! I hope you die and go to hell!'

After she had gone upstairs, I said to Jake, 'Let's go.'

'Where?' he asked.

'Away from here,' I said.

We went out of the house and walked silently but quickly over to Jake's car. He drove us to the willow tree. He broke a branch off the tree and hit its trunk with it all the while looking at me. Maybe this tree and this graveyard, with its broken outer wall and its decaying walkways, was where I belonged. At least the dead didn't lie. Then I randomly began to think about my grandparents on my Mum's side who I didn't know. They were buried round here, Henry and Ada, but I had never gone to their graves. 'Why didn't you tell me anything more about them than their names, Mum?' I asked inside.

We stood around for a while, and then I said, 'I'm going home. I want to be alone.' Jake walked with me to the gate of the graveyard.

'Are you alright, Kiran?'

I just kept walking. When we got to the gate, I started running. 'Let me drive you back, Kiran,' He shouted after me, 'please.'

I kept running, oblivious to the traffic. I was hungry all of a sudden. I searched my pockets, found a five-pound note and went to the chippy to get some food. Standing in the queue, I ignored someone asking me to let them see what I had under my hijab, and got myself some fish and chips and a drink and left the shop. I sat on a bench on the way home and ate, and as I ate, I sent a text to Dad: *I know the secret under the bed.* And shoving chips into my mouth I sent a text to Laila in Pakistan: *My Dad is in Pakistan, got another woman.*

I shoved more chips into my mouth, thinking about how I knew nothing about my Dad. How that smiling lump of hairy flab was a cold-hearted monster, going off to Pakistan just like that and marrying another woman. And then I hated Mum, for not telling me anything all my life. 'What happened to that baby, Mum?' I thought. 'And why didn't you tell me? If you had told me what had happened, what difference would it have made, Mum? And where is that baby now, Mum? Was he told a lie as well? Is that why I was invisible to you sometimes, or was it because you didn't want me, or was it because I didn't turn out white?'

I suddenly began to feel really, really sorry for Mum. 'Everything's out now, Mum,' I thought aloud, wrapping up what was left of my food; everything was out now. I made up my mind. I was going to go home and give Mum a great big hug, tell her I loved her, and tell her I understood, and give her all my love and make her come back to me. She was still my Mum and she was all I had left.

By the time I got home, it was dark. As I stepped through the front gate, I got a text from Dad: *Back today.*

A moment later, I got one from Laila: *On the plane with your Dad!*

The front door was slightly open. 'I must have forgotten to shut it,' I thought. The kitchen light was on and there was an empty bottle of vodka on the table. I didn't care if she was drunk; she was going to answer my questions. I called her as loudly as I could. She didn't answer.

Walking out of the kitchen, I saw a bloodstain on the floor. I called her again and followed the bloodstains. I rushed into the living room. She was lying on the sofa, her hand over the side of the arm. A knife lay on the floor, covered in blood.

I screamed. I touched her head, and she opened her eyes for a moment. I ran to the telephone and dialled 999. And then I called Jake. I held her bleeding arm up, and pressed on her cut. That's what she'd always said, 'Press on the cut. Stop it bleeding' - but it didn't. She opened her eyes again, then turned her head towards the coffee table and closed her eyes once more. There was a letter with my name on it.

The ambulance arrived before Jake. An ambulance woman took Mum's arm out of my hand, saying, 'Good girl.'

'Will she die?' I asked.

I don't know what the ambulance woman said in reply as just then old George, our neighbour, came into the room. The ambulance woman said something to him and he went out again and came back with a wet cloth from the kitchen.

'It's in God's hands, love,' George said, wiping my hands clean with the towel.

Mum was picked up, put on a stretcher and taken out of the house. I grabbed the letter Mum had written to me and followed her out.

'I'll lock up, love,' George told me. His dog, sitting in the yard, stared at me wagging its tail as I went past. The Browns looked out of their window and then drew their curtains. I got into the ambulance with Mum and we wailed off under the curious gaze of our street. As we were leaving, I saw Jake running towards our house.

Shamshad

Ya Allah, how could you let us sit there looking through each other for a couple of eternities. That is what we did. Just looked through each other. The wall clock hammered inside my head, in between the words of what Mum had just said. *I wish I was.* That's what she said. She wished she was my mother.

'Shamshad,' Mum said. 'It's not easy to say this.'

'And you think it is easy to listen to what you have to say to me,' I thought. I tried to blot out the ticking of the clock. I searched inside my head for a prayer to take the pain away. But what prayer was I going to find for the pain of my mother telling me she wished she was my mother?

I waited for Mum to tell whatever it was, but I really, really didn't want to know and yet still wanted her to quickly tell me - everything. She broke a piece of roti, dipped it in the daal and stirred it round and round and round, making a little whirlpool in her bowl.

After a lifetime, she dropped the roti into the daal and nodded up towards Dad's bedroom. She opened her mouth to speak, and I put my hands on my ears. The clock ticked louder and her words slashed into me. I could hear them clearly but they made no sense.

I went cold inside. I put my hands under the table, locked my fingers and bit my lower lip until it hurt.

'And you didn't want me,' I thought, cracking my fingers. I'm not stupid.

She put her face in her hands. Her *dupatta* slid off her head, went down the parting of her greying hair and fell onto her shoulders.

She said, looking up, 'He was once a very close friend of Liaqat, Kiran's Dad, Ghanzanfer's son. A long time ago, we went to Pakistan together. Me,' she nodded up towards Dad's bedroom, 'and him and Liaqat and his white wife. She had a baby with her, about a year old. A boy.'

I put my hands on the table. Flat, palms down.

Kiran

I was left on my own in the hospital's Accident & Emergency waiting room whilst Mum was whisked away. I texted Dad: *Mum in hospital. Tried to kill herself. Nearly dead. Hope you have a nice life with your new wife.*

I sent it.

I texted Laila: *Mum's tried to kill herself. Slashed her wrist. Nearly dead. In hospital…*

I sent it.

I wrote a text to Allah: *Give me back my Mum, Almighty. You have so many souls. You don't need a Mum. I need her.*

I searched for his name in my address book and kept looking for it until a policeman tapped me on the shoulder and asked me some questions about who I was and what had happened. He was still asking me questions when Jake came in. I moved away from the policeman.

'She's going to die,' I cried on Jake's shoulders.

He held me tightly. I felt his tears falling on my shoulders.

The ambulance woman who had brought us here came back from A&E. 'Will she die?' I asked her.

'Everything's being done that can be done for her, love,' the woman said, walking past me.

'Did she leave a letter?' the policeman asked.

I pulled it out of my jacket pocket. He put his hand forward to take it from me.

‘I haven’t read it yet,’ I said.

I sat down on a cold plastic chair with Jake next to me and opened Mum’s letter. Jake leaned over and read it with me. It said, in her beautifully neat handwriting:

My beloved Kiran. Don’t hate me. I love you. I have always loved you and whatever else I have done, I have never stopped loving you. I am not angry with you for opening my box. You had to know some day. But the pain, the pain, I can’t keep it down any more Don’t ever feel guilty. It’s not your fault.

Yes, I had a baby before you. I guess you know that anyway. His name was Ajmal. I had two miscarriages before I had him. When I was carrying him, I didn’t tell anyone, not even Lucky, until it was obvious.

And don’t hate Liaqat. He has raised you as a father should. He loves you. Always call him Dad. Always.

We went to Pakistan when Ajmal was just one year old. We were in the city near your Dad’s village. He wanted to sit on a tanga, a horse carriage. We were going to his uncle’s village. I said we should take a taxi. But he wouldn’t listen. We sat in the back, with Ajmal in my lap. I don’t know why it happened, maybe it was the road, it was all broken and full of holes. Suddenly, one of the wheels of the carriage came off. I was thrown out. Ajmal slipped out of my hands and fell onto the road on his head. He never woke up. He never cried. He just died. Right there. In my hands.

The funeral was so fast, too fast. I wanted to bring him back with me but couldn’t cope with the idea of him coming home, dead.

I will never forgive myself for taking him out there and leaving him there. I should not have buried him. He should have buried me. Just the thought of him kills me inside.

I want him back in my arms. I want to smell his breath and his voice, and for him to be next to me when I wake up in the middle of the night.

Years have gone by but a part of me still can't stop searching for him. I only have little pieces of him under my bed. I am not angry with you for what you did. I'm angry at myself for not knowing how to let go.

God knows how I've wanted to, so I can be there for you, but I just don't know how.

Jake put his trembling hand on mine.

Just then, I got a text from Dad: *Just arrived.*

A moment later I got a text from Laila: *Landed. Coming straight to you.*

Shamshad

Mum put a hand out towards me. I clenched my fists as her fingertips touched me.

She said, 'There was a terrible accident and the *goree* lost her baby. She sat by the baby's grave and cried and screamed day after day.' She paused, took a deep breath and continued, letting out a deep sigh, 'And there was a woman in the village, Khatija, a poor woman who worked in the house of the Choudrys, the big landlord of the village. He had made her pregnant. She was about to give birth and her offspring would be killed. Murdered. Everyone knew that.' Mum paused.

'Oh God, kill her now,' I thought, 'right in front of my eyes, I don't want to hear the rest.'

I tried to get out of the chair but couldn't.

Mum continued, 'The white woman was mad with grief. She wasn't going to live without her baby. On the night Khatija gave birth, all four of us were together, Liaqat and your Dad and me and her. And we stopped the murder.'

Mum paused again. I didn't see her getting up. She was now sitting next to me. She had her arm around me, holding me tightly. 'Khatija gave birth to twins. Two girls…'

'I hate you,' I cried. 'And don't tell me, me mother's your goat herder.'

Wiping my tears, Mum said, 'Shush, child, let me tell you everything.

'And the Choudry who fathered you was killed by his own son, Asmat Choudry, for what he had done. And I took you, and called you Shamshad. And your sister is called Kiran.'

I pushed her away and ran upstairs to my bedroom. She followed me. I slammed the door shut and locked it from inside. Rani was sleeping on my bed. She stood up, her body all erect. She jumped off and went under the bed. Mum knocked on the door, pleading for me to open it. I ignored her. I pulled a pair of scissors out of the drawer and looked at myself in the mirror. My dark–skinned face was hideous. I pulled my hijab off and ripped it up. I loosened my hair. Curly black snakes dangled over my shoulders.

'Open the door, Shamshad,' Mum called again and again.

Ignoring her, I chopped at the snakes and slashed my prayer mat.

I looked at my hand. My veins were throbbing. I had just put the blade of the scissors on my wrist when the door burst open. They were both there, *my Mum and my Dad.*

I gripped the scissors in my hand like a dagger.

She stepped forward, nodding, 'Stab me now. It is your right.'

And he stepped forward, fell to the ground and kissed my feet, saying, 'Do as you will to me.'

I raised my scissor-knife. My mobile rang. It rang and rang. I ignored it and clutched the scissors tighter. There was a text - from Laila. I stepped away and read it: *Kiran's Mum in hospital. Dying. Just landed. Will be there. I know everything.*

Dad stood up.

I put the scissors on the desk, showed him the text from Laila, and said, 'Take me to the hospital right now!'

Kiran

I got another text from Dad: *In taxi.*

I read more of Mum's letter.

All I could do was to live and relive the minutes, trying to wind the clock back, to get my Ajmal back, to leave this place and go home with my baby. Your father's village is a cruel place. In the village, there was a woman called Khatija, who had been made pregnant by a big, powerful man. Khatija gave birth to twins, two girls. They were going to be killed at birth, but we didn't let that happen. Liaqat and I took you and loved you. We named you Kiran, our light. And the other one, your sister, is called Shamshad, a shade for her family.

I don't understand fully why, but in that village a vow was taken, never ever to mention this. And I don't know why I went along with it for all those years. I should have stood up to them. Forgive me, my daughter.

'Could I please have the letter, young lady?' the policeman asked me.

I ignored him and read on.

And sometimes when I used to cry, it was not just for my baby. I cried for you not knowing, for me not knowing how to tell you, but also for the mother who lost two, from whom we took her babies. I know you must be hurting now and I ask you to forgive me. And tell your father I have always loved him and even as I write my last words, I still love him, but I can't live with all this pain any more. I love you and have always loved you. Mum.

I stood up and handed the policeman the letter.

A nurse called my name. Jake grabbed my hand and we went into the corridor. I searched the nurse's face to see if Mum had died. The nurse opened a door and Jake and I walked in.

'Is she dead?' I asked.

The nurse looked away from me, and said, 'The doctor is coming to see you,' and left.

A few moments later a doctor came in, his lips pursed.

'She has lost a lot of blood,' he told us. 'But she should be OK.'

'Should be or will be?' I asked. 'Can I see her, please?'

'She's asleep now. When she wakes up, we'll call you. Please stay in the waiting room.'

I prayed inside my head, 'Oh God save her, or I will never believe in you.'

At first, I couldn't believe my eyes when I saw her walking in through the main door of the hospital. Her hair was a mess, all chopped up. One side of it above her ears, the other on her shoulder. But it was Shamshad all right. When she saw me, she ran towards me, her arms open. Her Mum and Dad were behind her.

We hugged each other and cried.

'Kiran, I'm so sorry,' Shamshad said.

'So do you know?' I asked.

'Yes,' she said. 'It hurts.'

'I know,' I said.

'How's your Mum?' Shamshad asked.

'They said she'll be fine. She's sleeping now.'

'*Insha'Allah*, god willing,' Shamshad said.

'*Insha'Allah*,' I echoed.

Shamshad stepped back from me a little, wiped my face with her hand, and said, 'I hope so, Kiran, I really hope so.'

Jake gave Shamshad and me each a tissue. Shamshad closed her blood-shot eyes and wiped them. I took off my hijab and tried to put it on her head. She backed off, shaking her head.

I forced it on her head, asking, 'Who's older, you or me?'

'Me,' Shamshad smiled, adjusting her headscarf, 'probably.'

'No, you're just a big bully,' I laughed.

Shamshad's smile disappeared. She said, 'I said I'm sorry.'

'Just joking, sis.'

I got a text from Laila: *How's your Mum?*

I showed it to Shamshad, and then replied: *She'll pull through.* Laila replied: *B there in 2 mins.*

Then I got another one from Laila: *Love your Mum.* Then I got yet another one from Laila: *Mums!*

I showed the messages to Shamshad and we burst out laughing. 'What's so funny?' Jake asked, leaning towards us, trying to read the texts.

I showed him my mobile. He grinned.

Shamshad whispered in my ear, 'What's he doing here?'

'Shall we adopt him as a brother?' I whispered back.

Shamshad looked Jake up and down and said, 'Him, a *gora*!'

'What's up with you two?' Jake asked.

We didn't answer but just giggled.

Laila came in through the big swing doors of the entrance to the hospital. The Pakistan International Airlines tab was still on her handbag.

The three of us hugged.

Looking at Jake standing on his own not far from us, Laila exclaimed, 'Jake!'

Shamshad and I looked at each other, and then said together, 'Our brother!'

Jake blushed. He was about to say something when Laila interrupted with: 'And Jake, I heard a story about an English soldier who got captured and converted…'

'Converted!' Jake said. 'Dex? My brother! You must be mad.'

'I didn't say it was Dex,' Laila said.

'It can't be Dex, can it?' Jake asked.

Laila shrugged her shoulders. 'I said, I just heard a story.'

At that moment, Dad came in.

Hugging Laila, I saw the other woman with Dad. She was thin and dark.

'Is that what you left Mum for?' I thought.

Shamshad

A few moments after Laila came, Kiran's Dad walked in with the dark woman I had often seen on Skype. It was our mother. She was wearing a blue *shalwar kameez* suit and a thick brown jumper. Her cheeks were sunken, and she had deep dark patches under her eyes. Her arms were pressed into her side. The woman stood a few yards away from Kiran and me. Staring at us. She joined her hands and put them up to her face; she was trembling.

Kiran's Dad came up to me and put his hand on my head and stepped towards Kiran to hug her.

Pushing her Dad away from her, Kiran said, 'So you brought your wife with you to hospital, eh?'

Kiran

I thought Dad would get angry with me for what I had said to him, but he didn't. He looked at the dark woman, then at me and said, 'Kiran, this is your real mother.'

I felt faint. Shamshad put her arm around me and walked me towards our mother. Mother stepped back a little. She seemed to shrink, like a scared bird.

'*Ameejee*!' Shamshad cried. 'Mother.'

Mother kissed her hand and touched it to my face. Then she moved closer, stroked her hand down my face and then Shamshad's. She said something in Punjabi.

'She wants to know if we understand her language,' Shamshad explained to me.

Shamshad spoke a lot of words back to her. Mother shed heavier tears with each word. Turning to me, Shamshad said, 'I told her you can't.'

So many eyes were staring at us. A white man, with one arm in plaster and a bandage round his head, round his head, sneered at us: 'Does your whole tribe need to turn up if one of youse has got a headache?'

Jake turned to him so fast I thought he was going to hit him. But before Jake could do or say anything, Elizabeth from the East Boarhead Curry Club stepped in between the man and Jake. George and Mrs Bulldog were there as well. Elizabeth wasn't wearing her usual fancy clothes but George as ever was in his usual attire.

Pointing a finger straight at the face of the man with his arm in plaster, Elizabeth said, 'Beat it, you twat,' before I gob you one.' Nodding to Mrs Bulldog, Elizabeth added quickly, 'And then you'll 'ave Hilda to deal with.'

'Blimey, Liz, never thought you had it in yer to say sommet like this,' Hilda said.

'Leave it, it doesn't matter,' I said.

'It does,' George said.

The man with the injured arm lowered his head and walked out of the hospital.

Hilda went up to some people who were sitting in a corner and said something to them. They moved to other chairs, leaving four seats empty in a corner of the waiting room. Hilda came up to me and gave me a great big hug. She was still in her blue work clothes. I could smell the scent of baking biscuits on her. Shamshad, Mother, Laila and I sat down in the corner.

Dad was talking to a nurse. After he finished, he came over to me and said, 'Love you, Kiran. Let me see Sharon on my own for a bit, first.'

I nodded and he left.

Laila took out a cream-coloured scarf from her purse and gave it to me, saying, 'I bought this for you at Islamabad airport.'

'It's beautiful,' I said.

Mother looked us up and down, and she said something to Shamshad. 'Is she angry with me?' I asked Shamshad.

'No, Mother wants to know if *you* are angry with *her*?' Shamshad said. I shook my head.

Mother's face lit up with a massive smile. She spoke slowly, her words falling out of her mouth like flowers.

Shamshad translated as she spoke, 'There was never a day in which I didn't think of you both. There was never a night when I didn't dream of you. There was never a ray of light in which I didn't see my Kiran, and there was never a tree whose shade didn't remind me of my Shamshad. I knew your names. That's all I knew. And yes, I was angry, but with God, for giving me children the way he did. And then I was grateful to him for keeping you safe. And then I was angry with him for not letting me see you, even your faces, once, before today, not even a photograph. And now, I am the happiest mother on this earth, in front of whom shine the most beautiful jewels of this world.'

Dad came back and said to me, 'She's awake, you can see her.'

I looked at Mother. 'Go see her, Kiran, and give her my *salaam*. Tell her I prayed for her all the way through the flight.'

Shamshad translated for me.

'How does she know what Dad said?'

Shamshad asked asked Mother, who smiled and replied to Shamshad. 'She said the look on your face told her that the Almighty had listened to her prayers.'

Getting up to see Mum, I took hold of Dad's hand, and said to Shamshad, 'We're a *right* family, aren't we!'

Throwing a look at her Mum and Dad, who had stood at the side of the entrance to the hospital all this time, Shamshad replied, 'Aren't we just!'

When I went with Dad to see Mum, the East Boarhead Curry Club came along. A nurse stopped us, saying, 'Two at a time, please.'

'Give it a rest, luv,' Hilda replied to the nurse. 'We need to see our lass.'

The nurse stepped back and we went down a corridor and into a room. Mum had a tube in her nose. She was plugged into a machine, with all sorts of readings on small screens. Her eyes were shut. When Dad touched her hand, she opened her eyes and said in a weak voice, 'Liaqat.'

'It's Lucky, you daft git, and aren't I just, to get you back.'

Mum nodded to her curry club and nodded to me to come close to her. I did. She stroked the back of my hand with a finger and then closed her eyes again.

The way she closed her eyes filled me with terror. I thought she was dead, but the machines all kept on as they were.

Dad must have known what I was thinking. He said, 'Don't worry, she's just tired. They said she'll be home in a couple of days.'

We stood looking at Mum for a while. All the time, I kept thinking how lucky I was to have a family now with no secrets hidden under the bed, and to have discovered a brother, a sister and – then I smiled at the thought – two Mums.

Shamshad

After Kiran and her Dad went to see her Mum, Mother and I stood up and walked towards my Mum and Dad. When she got close to Mum, Mother sat on the floor and touched and tried to kiss my Dad's feet.

He quickly bent down and stopped her.

Mum helped Mother to her feet, saying, 'You must never do that again, never.'

'Can you forgive us?' Dad asked Mother.

'Can you?' Mum asked.

Turning to me, Dad asked, 'Can you forgive us, Shamshad?'

Mother flicked her shining eyes upwards, held her hands out and prayed, 'He is *Gafoor-ur-rahim*, the merciful, the forgiver. He has forgiven, who am I not to?'

Mum and Dad looked at me. I smiled back at them, thinking, 'Shamshad girl, you've got a lot of making up to do.'

And then I too held out my hands and repeated Mother's words: 'He is *Gafoor-ur-rahim*, the merciful, the forgiver. Ameen. He has forgiven, who am I not to?'